ENTICING LIAM

A BIG SKY ROYAL NOVEL

KRISTEN PROBY

AMPERSAND PUBLISHING, INC.

Enticing Liam
A Big Sky Royal Novel
By
Kristen Proby

ENTICING LIAM

A Big Sky Royal Novel

Kristen Proby

Cover Design: By Hang Le

Cover photo: Perrywinkle Photography

Published by Ampersand Publishing, Inc.

DEDICATION

For Montana – my home, not only by birth but also where my soul is on fire.

"I'm in love with Montana. For other states I have admiration, respect, recognition, even some affection. But with Montana it is love." – John Steinbeck

GLOSSARY

Who's who in Cunningham Falls…

Please know this may contain spoilers for anyone new to the series. The books each couple stars in is noted next to their description.

The King Family:

Jeff and Nancy King – Retired owners of the Lazy K Ranch. Parents of Josh and Zack King.

Josh King – Partner of Lazy K Ranch. Married to Cara Donovan. {Loving Cara}

Zack King – Partner of Lazy K Ranch. Married to Jillian Sullivan (Jillian is the sister of Ty Sullivan). Parents to Seth, Miles and Sarah. {Falling for Jillian}

Doug and Susan King – Doug is Jeff's brother. They live mostly in Arizona, but come to Montana in the summer. Parents of Noah and Grayson.

Noah King – Owner of Wild Wings Bird Sanctuary. Married to Fallon McCarthy, a yoga instructor and owner of Asana Yoga Studio. {Soaring With Fallon}

Grayson King – Ski Instructor on Whitetail Ski Resort. Married to Autumn O'Dea, a Pop music sensation. {Hold On, A Crossover Novella by Samantha Young}

The Sullivan Family:

Ty Sullivan – Attorney. Brother of Jillian. Married to Lauren Cunningham, a bestselling author, whose great grandfather first settled Cunningham Falls. Parents to Layla. {Seducing Lauren}

The Hull Family:

Brad Hull – Chief of Police. Married to Hannah Malone, an OB/GYN. {Charming Hannah}

Jenna Hull – Owner of Snow Wolf Lodge. Married to actor and superstar, Christian Wolfe. {Kissing Jenna}

Max Hull – Self-made billionaire. Married to Willa

Monroe (Sister to Jesse Anderson), owner of Dress It Up. Parents to Alex Monroe. {Waiting for Willa}

The Henderson Family:

Brooke Henderson – Owner of Brooke's Blooms. Married to Brody Chabot, architect. {Tempting Brooke, a 1001 Dark Nights Novella}

Maisey Henderson – Owner of Cake Nation. Married to Tucker McCloud, pro football player. {Nothing Without You, A Crossover Novella by Monica Murphy}

The Royal Family:

Prince Sebastian Wakefield – The Duke of Somerset. Married to Nina Wolfe (sister to Christian). {Enchanting Sebastian}

Prince Frederick Wakefield – Brother to Sebastian. Married to Catherine. No book belongs to this couple, as they are already married when introduced.

Prince Callum – Brother to Sebastian.

Princess Eleanor Wakefield – Sister to Sebastian. Married to Liam Cunningham. {Enticing Liam}

Jacob Baxter – Sebastian's best friend. Owner of Whitetail Mountain, along with several local businesses, including the restaurant Ciao. Married to Grace Douglas.

Liam Cunningham – Head of Montana security, and personal bodyguard to Sebastian. Cousin to Lauren Cunningham. Married to Ellie Wakefield. {Enticing Liam}

Nick Ferguson – Personal bodyguard to Nina Wolfe.

Miscellaneous and important characters:

Jesse Anderson - Former Navy deep-sea diver. Married to Tara Hunter. {Worth Fighting For, A Crossover Collection Novella by Laura Kaye}

Joslyn Meyers – Pop star. Married to Kynan McGrath. {Wicked Force, A Crossover Collection Novella by Sawyer Bennett}

Dr. Drake Merritt – Surgeon. Married to Abigail Darwin. Both characters are best friends of Hannah Malone. {Crazy Imperfect Love, A Crossover Collection Novella by K. L. Grayson}

Penelope (Penny) – Former teacher. Married to Trevor

Wood, Drummer for the rock band, Adrenaline. {All Stars Fall, A Crossover Collection Novella by Rachel Van Dyken}

Aspen Calhoun – New owner of Drips & Sips.

Sam Waters – Firefighter.

PROLOGUE

~LIAM~

"J ust landed," Phillip, who happens to be Princess Eleanor's personal security, says into my ear. I glance at the time.

Two in the goddamn morning.

"See you in ten." I hang up the phone and reach for my jeans. Usually, I would wear something more formal while on duty as the head of security for the royal family's Montana estate. But at two in the morning, the princess will have to deal with jeans and a T-shirt.

At least they're clean.

Six hours ago, I received a call from Phillip, giving me the heads-up that they were leaving London and headed here. But he requested I not tell Prince Sebastian, the man who pays my salary—and the eldest of the royal siblings.

Well, fuck that.

The prince is my boss, and in the past year that I've been employed here, we've established mutual trust and admiration.

His baby sister's random trip across the pond isn't a secret I plan to keep.

I jog from my apartment in the guesthouse of the lake-front property in Cunningham Falls, Montana, to the main residence. I key in the security code for the door and let myself in. I find Sebastian sitting in the kitchen, quietly reading something on his iPad.

"Good morning," I murmur and nod my head in a bow when he looks up at me. "Your Royal Highness."

"At this hour, you can call me Sebastian."

I feel my lips twitch. "Any idea why she decided to come all this way in the middle of the night?"

He shakes his head. "With Ellie, she could have just been in the mood for dinner at Ciao tomorrow."

I've met the princess a few times. She's a likeable woman. Beautiful. Smart.

Okay, so she's more than beautiful. She's stunning.

She's also a pain in my ass and almost died on my watch last summer, so I'd rather she not show up here at all. Especially when her trip is shrouded in secrets and drama.

Then again, maybe this is just Eleanor's life.

"The car will be here any minute," I inform Sebastian.

"You didn't have to come to the house."

"It's my job."

I receive a text, alerting me to the car pulling into the drive, and then walk to the entryway. Before anyone can knock, I open the door and look down into bright blue eyes.

"Hello, Princess."

Her mouth opens and closes, but she pulls herself together, lifts her chin into the air, and nods.

"Hello, Liam."

"Your brother is in the kitchen."

I step back to allow Eleanor and Phillip to enter the house, close the door behind them, and walk back to the kitchen in time to hear Eleanor say, "It was supposed to be a surprise."

She glares over at me, but I stand my ground and cross my arms over my chest.

"Keeping secrets from His Highness isn't what I'm paid to do."

"It wasn't a harmful secret," she mutters. "Well, surprise anyway."

"Hello, darling." Sebastian offers his sister a hug. "To what do we owe the pleasure?"

"Oh, you don't want to know, and I don't want to talk about it," she replies before sinking into a chair next to her brother. "Let's just say I needed a holiday. Far away from London."

"How long will you be staying?" Sebastian asks before I can.

"As long as possible. Maybe a couple of months."

I swallow the expletive before it crosses my lips.

3

A couple of months.

I trade a look with Phillip. "Will you be staying with her?"

"She's my charge," he says with a nod. "I go where she goes."

"You have a family in London," Eleanor reminds him. "You certainly don't have to stay. With Liam and Nick and the rest of Liam's team, I'll be safe."

"We'll discuss it," I say to Phillip. "If you don't need us any more tonight, we'll go back to headquarters."

"Go, get some rest," Sebastian says. "And thank you."

"Thank you," Eleanor echoes as Phillip and I walk out of the main house and down to HQ where the security team lives while on duty.

Nick—Sebastian's wife Nina's personal security— and I live here full time. The other team members live in town and work in shifts.

"You can take the second bedroom on the right upstairs," I inform Phillip.

"Thanks, but I'll be up now. Jet lag."

I nod. I rarely sleep myself. And now that Eleanor is on the property, I'll sleep even less. She has that effect on me. "Our first meeting will be at 0700."

CHAPTER 1

~ELLIE~

"*H*ello, Mummy." I grin at the face of my mother, who's holding the phone just a little too close for FaceTime. It seems whether you're royalty or not, the older generation struggles with technology.

I'm lying on the bed in the guest room with the phone propped on the pillows and my chin resting in my hands.

"I have your father with me," she says and turns the phone so I can see the king. "Say hello to Ellie, dear."

"Can you let Father hold the phone? He has longer arms, and I can see you both that way."

"I have it," Father says. Suddenly, both of my parents are in the frame.

"That's better. Hello to both of you."

"How are things in Montana?" Mum asks.

"Oh, it's beautiful here. Summer is lovely."

"Now that the pleasantries are out of the way," Father says, his brows lowering in a frown. "Why in the world did you sneak out of here without a word to anyone?"

"I had my security with me," I say in my defense. "I wasn't completely irresponsible."

"That didn't answer my question," he replies, and both of them wait silently for me to answer.

It won't do any good to lie. They'll find out eventually.

"Beau proposed to me," I admit, nausea at the very thought of it taking up residence in my belly. "Last week, the evening I left London."

"Oh, darling, that's wonderful," Mum says, but I shake my head.

"It's not wonderful. I don't love Beauregard. I don't even *like* him. He's pompous and rude. There's not a kind bone in that man's body."

"Well, then a simple no would have sufficed," Father says. "There was no need to flee the continent."

"Yes. There was." I swallow hard. "I know you love me very much, but I'm so tired of you trying to find me a suitable match. The men you try to set me up with are awful. They may have the right pedigree, but that doesn't make them good people."

"Britain is full of eligible men," Mum says. "You'll find one that suits."

"And sooner rather than later," Father says.

"I'm not an old maid."

"And you won't turn into one either," Father says. "I'll give you thirty days in Montana, but you'll come back in time for the state dinner next month. There will be plenty of eligible men there, and you have responsibilities."

Always with the responsibilities.

Everyone thinks that being a member of the royal household means dripping in jewelry and wearing pretty clothes and having the world served on a silver platter.

That is true, but it's *much* more than that.

"Yes, sir."

"Enjoy your time with Sebastian and Nina," Mum says. "And please send them our love."

"I will." I offer them a cheerful smile. "And I'll be home in time for the dinner."

"Goodbye, daughter," Father says.

"Goodbye."

I hang up the phone and let out a deep sigh, then toss my cell on the bed and roll onto my back, staring at the ceiling. My parents don't understand. They met when my mother was in her early twenties and have been inseparable since.

It's rather difficult to find the man you're supposed to spend the next seventy years with when you're under this kind of pressure.

Fortunately, I don't have to think about that right now. I have thirty days to relax. And thankfully, Sebastian and Nina haven't tried to pry into why I came here so abruptly. They've given me space to sleep, read, and daydream.

This lake house is perfect for all of those things. At more than ten-thousand square feet, there is plenty of room to be alone. But I know that if and when I want their company, I'm always welcome to join them.

I walk into the closet and choose a sundress for the day, slip my feet into Hermes slides, and walk down to the main living area where we usually congregate. Nina's spreading something on a bagel. Nick is outside on the deck, close enough to see Nina but out of earshot.

Sebastian and the other security members are nowhere to be seen.

"Where is everyone?" I ask as I reach for a banana and sit at the island. I love how open the kitchen is to the rest of the living space, and how from anywhere in the room, a person can look out the floor-to-ceiling windows to the lake beyond.

"They're in a meeting," Nina says with a smile. "Would you like a bagel and cream cheese?"

"I'll share it with you," I offer, and Nina happily slides half of her breakfast over to me. "Thank you. What kind of meeting?"

"Well, since you've been here for a week and we don't know how long you're staying, the security team is trying to decide if Phillip should stay or go, and what to do if he goes."

"Where are they?" I set the bagel down and stand from the chair.

"In the guest house," she replies and frowns. "Tell Nick if you're planning to go down there."

"It's twenty yards away."

She narrows her eyes. "Ellie, you're my sister-in-law, and I love you, but you know what happened when we rebelled against the rules."

"I almost died," I murmur. "Fine, I'll tell him."

I walk to the glass door and crack it open. "Nick? I'm going to head down to the guest house."

"I'll let them know," he says and speaks into a device on his wrist. "The sparrow is headed to HQ."

I close the door and smile at Nina. "See? I follow the rules."

Nina laughs and takes a bite of her bagel. "Want me to come with you?"

"No need. I'm here for thirty days. I'm going to let them know."

I wave at her and walk through the house to the door closest to the guest house. As I step outside, I see Phillip walking up the path.

"I'm capable of walking twenty yards without an armed guard. Especially here."

"Humor me," he says and escorts me to the house. He opens the door for me, and when I step inside, I'm met with more testosterone in one room than should be legal.

It's a *lot*.

"What is it, Ellie?" Sebastian asks after the men all stand and bow their heads to me.

"I'm staying for thirty days," I announce. "I understand this meeting is about how to *handle* me, and I'm updating you of my plans."

Liam frowns and glances down at the paper on the table in front of him.

"Is that a problem?" I ask him.

"Your Highness," Phillip begins, "we were just discussing whether I should stay or go back to London. I would usually stay with you wherever you are in the world. That's my job, of course."

"You've been with me for ten years, Phillip. Just tell me what's wrong."

"My wife is about to have our second child any day, Highness. I'd rather not miss it, but—"

"You didn't tell me she's expecting," I interrupt and break protocol long enough to lay my hand on Phillip's shoulder. We never touch our employees, but I consider Phillip a friend. "Of course, you should go. Today. Straight away. And please, keep me posted on how Cynthia and the baby are doing. Send photos. You know I love babies."

Phillip smiles kindly at me. "Thank you, but it's not that easy."

"Why ever not?" I look around the room with a frown. "There are eight men in this room, not counting my brother, each who are more than capable of looking after me. I'm not a troublemaker."

Liam smirks, and I narrow my eyes on him. "Do you have something to say?"

Liam starts to speak, but Sebastian interrupts. "Nick and Liam have full-time assignments," he says. "The other men are assigned to the house in shifts. So, we're looking at manpower and who to assign to you in Phillip's absence."

I nod. "I understand, and this isn't my area of expertise." I watch Liam as I speak. "I just wanted to give you the information."

I turn to leave, but Liam stops me. "Thank you, Your Highness."

I nod and continue out the door, marching back to the big house. I've been attracted to Liam since I first laid eyes on him last year.

He's tall, dark, and mysterious. He looks dangerous. He's sexy as can be, and I don't have much experience when it comes to men. So, whenever I'm around him, I feel like a bumbling idiot.

Ah, well, at least he's not assigned to me. I'll just stay out of his way, and everything will be fine.

"WHAT DO you mean Liam's assigned to me?" I demand, staring at my brother as if he's daft. "Liam is *your* personal security."

"Charles is coming to Montana," Sebastian replies calmly. Charles has been around since I was in nappies.

But Liam's in charge of the Montana property. "Phillip is leaving this evening after Charles arrives, and Liam will be assigned to you for the duration of your stay."

I glance at Nina, who hasn't said a word. "Don't look at me."

"Why is this a problem?" Sebastian asks.

"It's not. It's just a surprise."

I have to be around Liam 24/7 for the next thirty days? My sex-deprived body might spontaneously combust.

"What am I missing?" Sebastian asks Nina, who just shakes her head innocently.

"You're not missing anything."

Thank God for Nina. She knows I have a crush on Liam. But I can behave professionally.

I've been doing it for over twenty-five years.

And I know better than to try and stick my nose into our security team's business. They're here to keep me safe.

"So starting tomorrow, then?"

Sebastian nods.

"Oh, also, there's a girls' night out planned for tomorrow night at Brooke's Blooms," Nina says. "We're going to eat delicious cake and learn how to arrange pretty summer flowers. Please join us, Ellie."

Butterflies fill my belly. "Of course, I will. That sounds like so much fun."

"Excellent."

Being a royal has always been lonely for me. I have

my siblings, but they're all older, living their lives. And I've had nannies, of course.

But I've been lacking any real, true friendships.

Until I met Nina and all of her wonderful friends in Montana. They include me as if it's the most natural thing in the world to do.

And I'm grateful.

"I think I'll go down to the dock and read."

"No boating," Sebastian says.

"Trust me, I have no plans to get on a boat ever again." I fetch my sunglasses and my book, stop at the fridge for a can of Coke, and walk down to the dock that juts out from the boathouse—which is large in its own right. There is an apartment in it, above the lift for the boats. At the corner of the dock is a small covered area with seating. It's perfect for lounging with a book and watching the water.

Phillip stands by the boathouse, watching the water and taking in our surroundings, always alert. I feel awful that I didn't know about his wife's pregnancy. And due any day besides. I would have made other arrangements when I came to Montana last week had I known.

It's good that Phillip is going back to London this evening. But now I'll have Liam stuck to me like glue for the next four weeks.

Not that looking at him is a hardship. He can be curt with me, but I probably deserve it.

Especially after last year. I was going through a bit of a rebellious phase.

One near-death experience was enough to pull me out of that stupidity.

Liam's never forgiven me, though. Perhaps I'll be able to have a conversation with him over the next couple of days. I'll apologize and clear the air.

With a plan in place, I open my book and settle in for a lazy afternoon near the water.

CHAPTER 2

~ELLIE~

"*A*re you saying you don't want me here?" I frown at my sister-in-law as she shakes her head back and forth, her pretty blond hair swaying with the movement.

"Not at all," she insists. "You know I *love* having you here. But the boathouse is more private for you."

"You're going to be here for a month," Sebastian adds. "We were trying to be sensitive to your privacy. The apartment out there is empty but still on the property, so there's no issue for security."

I'm sitting in the living room of Sebastian's home, staring out the windows at the boathouse below. I've never had the opportunity to stay somewhere detached from the palace or the primary residence of wherever we were staying.

The idea of having more privacy takes root, and I

find myself nodding in agreement. "Can we go down and have a peek?"

"Of course," Nina says, jumping up from the couch. We walk down to the door leading outside and find Nick waiting for us.

So far, I haven't seen Liam at all today, but I also haven't had to leave the house. Thanks to modern technology, we can be monitored easily from the guest house where the security team is stationed.

Charles arrived last evening, and Phillip left straight away, so as of right now, I'm Liam's charge.

"Ellie and I are going down to the boathouse," Nina informs Nick as we walk past him and down the path to the dock that leads to the boathouse door. Nick follows not far behind. "I've already redecorated this space," she says.

We enter the boathouse and climb a set of stairs that leads to an open room.

"Oh, this is beautiful."

"As you can see, I love Joanna Gaines," Nina says with a laugh.

The space is painted white with light grey wood floors. The small kitchen is open to the living area, and the space is decorated with colorful rugs and pillows. A couch and a chair face a television, the living area adjacent to a small dining room, and the windows facing the water are huge.

"That view is spectacular."

"Trust me, I've thought of moving out here myself,"

Nina says. "It's quiet, the apartment is cute, and the view can't be beat. Also, check this out."

She walks to the wall of windows. To my surprise, she pulls open the glass and leads me out onto a wide deck.

I could live here for the rest of my days. With the lake and the mountains, it's the most beautiful view I've ever seen.

"Wow."

"I know," Nina says. "Come on, I'll show you the bedroom."

We walk back inside, and she shows me the master suite with its attached bathroom. There's a soaking tub that has my name written all over it.

With another half-bath for guests, Nina has thought of everything.

"I absolutely want to stay out here," I say once the tour is finished. "It's completely perfect for me."

"So, you don't think I'm trying to get rid of you?" she asks.

"No. You're right, I'll be happy out here. Not that the house isn't wonderful, but some alone time is exactly what I need."

"I thought so." Nina hugs me close and then holds my hand as we step back out onto the deck. "I know you came here because you were running from something. Or someone."

I glance her way, but she just shrugs a shoulder.

"You'll talk about it when you're ready. But I know

how it feels to need some space. You'll get that out here."

"Thank you." I rest my head on Nina's shoulder. "Thank you so much."

"You're welcome."

"Where do you want these things?"

We turn at Liam's voice and see him standing in the living room, holding my bags.

"Oh, in the bedroom," I say.

"For the record," he says after he sets my things in the bedroom and returns, "I'm not in favor of this arrangement."

"Why not?" I ask, watching his handsome face. His jaw is set, his brown eyes hard as he props his hands on his hips and stares at me.

He's the least formal of all the security that's ever been with us. It's not that he's careless. Or not good at his job.

He's just not as formal as I'm used to. He rarely bows when he sees us, and he hardly ever calls me *Your Highness.*

It's protocol and what I'm used to.

But Liam doesn't bother me in the least.

"Because the boathouse isn't as protected as the other areas of the property. It's exposed to the lake, which means if someone wants to get to you, they can try from the water."

"The odds of that are—"

"Small but not non-existent." He licks his lips and paces the kitchen, clearly agitated.

"There are cameras outside," Nina says, trying to be reasonable. "And boat surveillance, as well. Ellie is perfectly safe here."

Liam is quiet for a moment, seeming to think it over. "We will make it work. *Please*, Your Highness, don't leave the property unless I'm with you."

"I understand," I reply. "I won't pull a stunt like last year again, Liam. You have my word on that."

He nods once and then leaves Nina and me alone in the boathouse.

"Do you still think he's hot?" Nina asks quietly.

He's bloody amazing.

"He's an attractive man," I reply, trying to sound cool. "If you like the tall, dark, and dangerous type."

Nina laughs and slings her arm around my shoulders. "We all do, friend. We all do."

"If I eat another bite of this cake," Nina says later in the evening, "I'll die from the sugar rush."

We're at Brooke's Blooms in downtown Cunningham Falls with most of what I've started to call *the gang*. Nina's friends—and now mine, as well—are Jenna, Willa, Hannah, Grace, and Fallon. Some are related by marriage, but all are wonderful friends who have welcomed me into the fold. I feel as if I've been here all of my life.

At first, I was terribly intimidated by them because I'm younger, and all of these women have successful careers and families.

But they've never made me feel anything but included and happy to be amongst them.

"How long are you staying, Ellie?" Willa asks as she tries to fit a rose into the middle of her bouquet. This flower class that Brooke offers is wonderful. She and her sister, Maisey, feed us all the cake we could ever want, and also have wine and a charcuterie table set up.

We'll all leave with our bellies full and our hands bursting with flowers.

Not to mention, if I keep drinking wine at the pace I've been going, more than a little pissed.

"About a month," I answer and raise my glass when Maisey offers to pour me a refill. "I need to be back in London for a state dinner at the end of next month."

"Sebastian and I will be there for that, as well," Nina says. "So, I'll get to see even more of you."

I smile at Nina and clap my hands in excitement. "Brilliant! I haven't seen enough of you lately."

"We're always going here and there," Nina says. "It seems we never stay in one spot for more than a week at a time."

"But you get to see such exciting places," Hannah reminds Nina. "Brad and I are so entrenched in this community—which I'm not complaining about—but we never have time to go anywhere."

"What would Cunningham Falls do without their chief of police and the best OB/GYN in town?" Fallon asks and takes a bite of her cake. "Maisey, this gluten-free cake is *so good*. It tastes like regular cake."

"Oh, thank God," Maisey says with a relieved sigh. "I've been tweaking that recipe, and you're the first to try it. Do you really like it?"

"It's fabulous," Fallon assures her.

I glance to my left where Liam and Nick flank the door, both standing stoically. I'm used to having security with me.

I'm not used to having *Liam* so close to me all the time.

"Would you two like some cake?" Willa asks the men.

"No, ma'am," Liam replies.

"You love cake," Jenna says, frowning at Liam.

I glance around, surprised. "Do you know each other?"

"Jenna and I are a little younger than Liam, but we were friends with Lauren Cunningham—"

"Sullivan now," Fallon reminds her. "She's married to Ty Sullivan."

"Right," Willa says with a nod. "Lauren and Liam are cousins, and he came to Cunningham Falls for the summers."

That part, I knew. Liam told me that when I first

met him and cornered him at Sebastian's house, hoping to flirt with him a bit.

Of course, I'm absolutely abysmal when it comes to flirting.

"And he always *loved* sweets," Jenna adds.

"We're on duty," Liam reminds her.

"I'll send some home with you," Maisey says. "I have plenty, and you can enjoy it when you're *not* on duty."

"Thank you," Nick says with a smile, then assumes his stoic stance once again.

"My flowers look like a drunk elephant put them together." I stare at my pitiful bouquet in disgust.

"You *are* a little drunk," Nina says. "Your cheeks are bright red."

"That always happens." I cover my face with my hands and laugh. "Not that I have the opportunity to over-indulge often, but my flushed cheeks always give me away."

"You're adorable." Grace, who has been quiet up until now, leans over to tap my glass with hers. "I like you."

"I like you, too." I blink rapidly, not wanting to become a blubbering idiot over some sweet words. "I must have something in my eye."

We spend the next hour putting the finishing touches on our flowers and polishing off our cake and wine. When Nick and Liam escort Nina and me out to our waiting car, I find myself stumbling over my feet.

Liam immediately reaches out to grab my elbow to keep me upright.

"Pardon me," I say, trying to sound proper. "That sidewalk snuck right up on me."

"Or the wine did," Nina says with a snort. "That was fun. We need to do it more often."

We climb into the back seat, and I sigh in happiness. I'm completely hammered. I don't remember the last time I drank in such excess.

Perhaps never. It would be frowned upon to behave in such a way back home.

"Don't feel guilty," Nina says as if she can read my thoughts. "It's time you act twenty-five."

"I *am* twenty-five," I remind her.

"Exactly."

The car pulls into Sebastian's drive, and Nick escorts Nina inside the house.

"Let's go, Princess," Liam says, motioning for me to walk down the path that winds beside the house to the lake below.

"Where are you taking me?"

"To your apartment," he says, his lips twitching with humor. I want to kiss those lips. I've wanted to kiss them since the day I first met him.

"Oh, right. I almost forgot." I giggle as I walk on the path next to Liam. When I stumble, he reaches out for me again.

I *really* like it when Liam touches me.

It makes my skin tingle.

I rub my lips together, hoping that will keep me from babbling. Alcohol gives me loose lips.

It's a curse.

"It's hot tonight." I wipe my brow with the back of my hand. "Is it always so hot here in the summer?"

"Yes."

I frown at him. "You're not much for chatting, are you?"

"No."

I narrow my eyes, still watching him. Well, both of him. "You're allowed to speak to me, you know."

"Okay."

My toe catches on something, pitching me forward, but before I can land face-first on the path, Liam's arms encircle my middle, holding me up.

"Oops."

"Do I need to carry you, Princess?" He sounds angry. Frustrated. I don't know why, this is his bloody job.

"I can walk."

I think.

When he sees that I'm stable once again, he takes his hands away. Despite the hot evening, my skin is cool where his hands were.

I'm a bloody hormonal mess.

Liam is too virile for his own good.

We make it safely to the dock and the boathouse. Liam opens the door, and I step inside. To my surprise, he helps me up the stairs.

"I can do it," I mumble.

"You'll fall on your face," he mutters.

Once at the top, I grin. "See? We made it!"

But my damn toe catches on something else. This time, I hit the floor.

"How many glasses of wine did you have?"

"Good question. I didn't count. A lot. You can go, I'll be fine."

"Like hell." He pulls me up, and suddenly, I'm pressed against him from hip to chest, looking up into his brown eyes. His jaw is firm, his lips pressed into a hard line.

"I'm a virgin."

I feel my eyes grow wide, but I suddenly can't stop talking.

"I know it's silly, but I'm a twenty-five-year-old virgin. Can you believe that?"

"Uh—"

"Absolutely ridiculous," I mutter and let my eyes travel down to his neck, where his Adam's apple bobs as he swallows hard. "And you're an attractive man, Liam."

"I should go."

"No way." I grip his shoulders. He could easily push me away, but he doesn't, and I take that as a good sign. "I don't know why I'm telling you this. Wait. Yes, I do. I'm telling you because I think you're attractive, and I like it when you touch me, and maybe you should teach me all about the sex."

"Christ," he mutters and closes his eyes. "*The* sex?"

"Yes. I'm here for a month, and you're here with me. It's convenient."

"No."

"But why?" I sound whiny, even to my own ears.

"Because I work for you."

"You work for my *brother.* Not me."

"No."

"But why?"

"Because you're too young for me."

"I'm a grown woman who can make her own decisions with her body, thank you very much." I hiccup and do my best to look sophisticated.

"No."

"But why?"

"For a million other reasons that make this a very bad idea."

I frown and bite my numb lip, still staring at Liam's Adam's apple.

"Why do they call this an Adam's apple?" I brush my finger down the firm bump in his neck.

"I don't know."

"Me either." I smile up at him. "I've never even had an *orgasm*, Liam. Isn't that just preposterous? Some women can do...things...to themselves to make it happen, but I don't know how to do that. I would Google it, but all of my internet usage is monitored. All the time. Can you imagine being called into the king's office because I've been caught looking at internet porn?"

"No."

"But why?"

"I swear to God, Eleanor, I'm not going to say it again."

"Are you going to sue us for sexual harassment?"

"No." He laughs and grips my upper arms to push me back from him.

"I quite liked where I was."

"Me, too," he grumbles. "And this can't happen."

"Of course." I shake my head. "I'm doomed to be a virgin forever. Because the men I've met are all complete arseholes. Especially that mean Beauregard. He thought he could bully his way into being my husband and have a place in the royal household.

"Made him real mad when I wouldn't let him in my knickers, I'll tell you that."

"I'll make a note to have him killed." Liam's voice isn't light and full of humor.

His eyes are fierce. His jaw clenched.

"Are you angry on my behalf, Liam Cunningham?"

He doesn't reply, just watches me with that intense look on his impossibly handsome face.

"You have a scar, right here," he says, reaching out to point to my jawline, but he doesn't touch me.

"I fell when I was small. I have three older brothers. They always got me into trouble."

Liam nods. "You should go sleep off that wine."

27

"Yeah." I sigh, resigned to going to bed by myself. "I'll stop hitting on you now."

I take a step. "Wait!" I whirl back around and brace myself on a chair so I don't fall again. "I have to apologize."

"For what?"

"For last summer. For the stunt I pulled that put so many of us in danger. I didn't mean for anyone to get hurt."

"I know."

"It was stupid and thoughtless, and I want to let you know that it won't happen again."

"You've apologized before."

"I know, but I feel like you haven't forgiven me, and that's why you're not very nice to me. Anyway, goodnight."

I turn to walk to the bedroom, immediately pulling the glittery tank I wore to the party over my head and letting it fall to the floor.

I don't even give the fact that I'm not wearing a bra a second thought.

"Jesus," Liam says behind me.

"What?"

"Don't turn around," he says quickly. "Go to bed, Ellie."

"Yes, sir."

∾

I'M DYING.

I moan and roll onto my back, take a deep breath, and then shove my face back into the pillow.

Yep, I'm dying. Probably of alcohol poisoning. My head feels like it's split in two, my stomach roiling. I swear I've eaten a whole handful of cotton balls.

I want to just lie here all day, but I have to wee like crazy, and my phone has been buzzing with messages.

That's what woke me.

I have no idea what time it is, and I'd look, except with my head cracked open, I'm quite sure I've gone blind.

I stumble my way into the loo, and once I've done my business, washed my hands and face, and scooped my hair into a knot on the top of my head, the headache starts to abate.

I pull on some yoga shorts and a sports tank, then pad out to the kitchen for a glass of water.

I stumble into a chair, sending it crashing to the floor. Grateful that it wasn't *me* landing in a heap, I pick it up and pour myself a glass of water.

"Are you okay up there?"

Liam appears at the top of the steps. His eyes roam over me from head to toe.

"It was a chair," I reply and sit on the couch, pulling my feet up under me. I lean on the arm of the sofa. "I'm dying."

"You had a bit to drink last night."

"Yeah. Or a lot."

I sip the water, hoping it'll settle my stomach.

Images start to fill my mind, and I frown.

"You know, I had a crazy dream that I told you some of my secrets."

"That wasn't a dream."

Liam sits in the chair across from me, braces his arms on his knees, and frowns.

"Wait, it wasn't?"

"No."

No.

He told me no several times.

Because I practically begged him to shag me.

I let my head fall back onto the couch. "Bloody hell."

CHAPTER 3

~ L I A M ~

*S*he's the sexiest damn thing I've ever seen in my whole godforsaken life. Even with the tousled hair and smeared makeup. And in that barely-there outfit, it's taking all the strength in me not to reach out and touch her soft skin.

But she's off-limits. Without a doubt, no questions asked, off-limits.

"Wait." Eleanor's head whips up, and she stares at me with wide, hopeful eyes. "Did you end up saying yes?"

I slowly shake my head from side to side. "No."

She lets her head fall back again and mutters, "Damn."

"Eleanor—"

"No." She holds up a hand and lifts her head so she can level me with narrowed blue eyes. "We're talking about sex and nakedness. I think you can call me Ellie. Not Your Highness or Princess or Eleanor."

"Ellie." I clear my throat. "You don't really want what you're asking."

She smirks and pulls a knee up to her chest. For protection or because of nervousness, I'm not sure. "Because I'm young, and I don't know my own mind?"

This is a trick question. "No, because you don't know *me*, and I'm telling you, I'm not the man who should be teaching you about these things. You should find someone kinder, softer. Gentler."

"Well, that sounds bloody boring," she counters and then tips her head to the side. "I may be inexperienced, but I'm not stupid, Liam. I'm old enough to know myself and what I want."

"And you think that's me."

She licks her lips, and it's almost my undoing. Ellie has the kind of lips you don't just want to kiss. You want to explore them. Bite. Sink in and live there for a few good hours because the glories that a man is sure to discover and experience are endless.

Her curves turn me inside out. Her hair is thick and begs to be twisted around my fingers.

And that view I got of her bare back last night kept me up into the wee hours of the morning with a hard-on that rivaled granite.

I want her.

But I'm not right for her. That I know for sure. I've seen too much. Done horrible things.

None of that should ever touch her.

Ellie leans forward and keeps her eyes steady on mine. "I haven't made it a secret since the day I met you that I find you attractive, Liam. Yes, I want you. But I'm not a child, and you said no. So, the answer is no. Don't worry, we won't have any issues."

That's the right answer. I should nod and go about my day, leave it in the past, forget it ever happened.

But I can't ignore the look of hurt in her eyes. She's put on a brave face, but I see the pain all the same.

I don't want to hurt Ellie—or anyone for that matter. But I'm not the right man for her to tumble into bed with.

I have a job to do.

"I have a nail appointment in an hour," she says, ending the conversation. "I'll be down in forty-five minutes."

She's dismissed me. I nod and stand, then walk toward the stairs leading down to the door.

"She okay?"

I turn to find Nina smiling, holding a basket of pastries.

"Yes, ma'am."

"Well, I have a headache the size of Beverly Hills," she says with a wince. "That'll teach me to drink too much wine. Muffin?"

"No, thanks."

"I wish you guys would eat more," she mutters as

she walks through the door. Before it closes, I hear her call out, "I bring food!"

I have things to do in headquarters before I take Ellie to her appointment. I need to consult with Charles on a few things, and I have some paperwork to see to.

But Ellie is always at the forefront of my mind.

"OH, WHAT A CUTE LITTLE SHOP," Ellie says as I park in front of a salon called *The Style Studio*. It's next door to Asana Yoga Studio, with a girly front window full of fussy things and signs advertising hair, nails, and lash services. "I never get to go out for this kind of thing. My nail and hair techs always come to the palace for me. This is a treat."

"What do people do to their lashes?" I can't help but ask.

"Extensions, lifting, color," Ellie lists as she gathers her bag, and I get out to then open her door. She smiles up at me. "Do you like mine?"

"Your lashes?"

"Yes." She flutters them for my benefit.

"They're not real?"

She chuckles and shrugs a shoulder. "Well, mine are in there, but I do have extensions. I keep them light and natural, but it's awesome because I rarely have to wear mascara, and if I don't want to wear makeup at all, it's no big deal."

I stare at her, blinking slowly.

"I've lost you," she guesses.

"Being a woman is damn complicated."

Ellie laughs at me, and I hold the salon door open for her. We both walk in.

It smells like chemicals. Music plays through invisible speakers. There are four hair stations, two nail stations, and a receptionist's desk.

"I'm Ellie," Ellie tells the receptionist.

"Of course. Welcome, Your Highness." The young girl smiles politely. "I have you down for a manicure and a blowout."

"That's right."

I step back and keep an eye on the shop as Ellie's shown to a seat at one of the nail stations.

Aspen Calhoun, the new owner of Drips & Sips, is getting her hair cut nearby and smiles and says hello to Ellie. They're deep in conversation when I see my cousin, Lauren, walk through a door in the back of the room.

"Liam," she says with a happy smile and offers me a hug. "Let me just pay for my facial, and we'll chat."

Lauren turns to the receptionist, settles her bill, and then turns back to me. "Let's step out."

I glance around the room once more. "I'll be right outside," I say to Ellie, who eyes Lauren but nods to me.

I follow my cousin out to the sidewalk. It's warm

again today, but the walk is covered, making it comfortable.

"I've barely seen you since you moved here," Lauren says.

"It's been busy, working for the royal family and all that." I reach out and tug on a strand of her hair, the way I've done since we were kids. "How are you?"

"I'm great. Layla is starting school this fall, and Asa is going to preschool a few days, as well, so I'll have some quiet time to write."

"And how's Ty?"

Lauren married Ty almost six years ago. I like him a lot. Much better than her bastard of a first husband.

"Busy. His law practice is doing better than ever."

"I'm glad you're doing so well. You deserve it."

"Now, tell me about you."

I frown. "You know everything. I work. That's it."

"And her?" Lauren gestures at the window to where Ellie is sitting inside.

"She's my job."

"Well, the way she looked me over just now tells me she'd like to be more than that."

I shake my head. "That's not how it is."

Lauren pats my shoulder. "I know. You're stubborn and have a ridiculous work ethic. But don't forget to actually *live* your life, Liam. You know better than anyone how short it can be."

In more ways than I want to admit or think about.

"Come to dinner at our house," Lauren suggests.

"I'm stuck to her like glue for the next month. There's no time off."

She rolls her eyes. "Bring her with you. I'm sure she's nice, and our house is safe. Well, from assassins anyway. I can't guarantee you won't step on a lego."

"Liam."

Ty hurries up beside Lauren, slips his arm around her waist, and holds his hand out for mine.

"Hey, good to see you."

"We're grabbing lunch," Ty says. "Join us?"

"I'm working," I reply. "But thanks."

"I told him he should come by for dinner," Lauren says. "And I also told him to bring Princess Eleanor with him."

Ty's eyebrows climb. "Sure. Anytime. We're grilling steaks tomorrow night. Come on over."

"I'll think about it."

That's code for *no*.

Not that I care if my family meets Ellie. That's not it at all. But I don't want her to think it's a date.

We're not dating.

"There's no thinking. You're coming." Lauren pats my shoulder again. "See you tomorrow. Six o'clock. If you don't show up, I'll come find you."

"I don't remember you being such a bully."

My cousin laughs. "I miss you. So, come to dinner. Okay?"

I nod, not wanting to say yes when I can't make any promises.

I stay outside after Lauren and Ty leave, keeping an eye on the passersby, breathing in the fresh, summer air.

I love Cunningham Falls. My great-grandfather helped to establish the town more than a hundred years ago. My father and Lauren's father are—or *were*—brothers. Lauren's parents died ten years ago, and it was a hard blow to our entire family.

Although my parents moved my sister and me away from Cunningham Falls when we were young so my dad could pursue a job in Seattle, we came back here every summer. For three glorious months, we lived at Lauren's house, swam in Whitetail Lake, and rode our bikes all over town.

I knew that once I was out of the Army, I'd move here someday. It's where I seem to be the most at peace. And for a man who barely remembers what that feels like, it's absolute heaven.

"All done," Ellie announces as she walks through the door. "I just met the most wonderful women. Aspen owns Drips & Sips, and she's *so* funny. Just lovely. I wish my hair was naturally red like hers.

"She introduced me to her hairstylist, Monica, and my nail girl is Natasha. They're all so nice. I'm absolutely coming back here. It's brilliant."

"I'm glad you had a good time."

"Who was the woman you were talking to?"

I open the car door for her, then climb into the driver's seat.

"Not that it's any of my business," she adds. "Forget I asked."

I should. I should forget she asked and let her think Lauren is someone I'm interested in.

But I'm not a liar.

"That was my cousin, Lauren."

Ellie's eyes widen. "Oh, I would have loved to meet her."

"Well, you might get the chance." I tell her about the dinner invitation.

"Of course, you should go," she says.

"I'm working. With you."

"I'm safe at home," she argues. "You can certainly take a few hours off to enjoy your family. You can't work twenty-four hours a day, and the last time I checked, no one requires that of you."

She's not wrong. But I don't trust anyone to protect Ellie the way I can.

"But since she invited me, I'd like to come along."

And there it is.

"Are you sure?"

"Oh, absolutely. What should I take as a hostess gift? Flowers seem impersonal, but I don't know her yet. Perhaps a bouquet and a nice bottle of wine. I'll see what Sebastian has in the wine cellar."

I'm absolutely *not* dating her. I refuse to touch her.

But she's coming to meet my family.

Fucking perfect.

~

"DON'T TAKE ME HOME YET," Ellie says, surprising me.

"Where do you want to go?"

"Let's go for a walk," she suggests.

"You're not really wearing hiking shoes."

"I said a walk, not a hike."

Pioneer Park, over by Lauren's house, has paved walking paths that should be fine on Ellie's feet, so I turn toward that side of town. I park in the lot and open her door for her.

"I'll be close," I say.

"Come walk with me, Liam," she replies. "It's just a bloody stroll."

I fall into step next to her, my eyes always skimming over the people nearby, the vehicles in the lot, looking for anything suspicious.

"We're in a park in Montana," Ellie says with a sigh. "I hardly think someone will try to kidnap or harm me here."

"You never know," I mutter. "I'm doing my job."

"I know. And I'm grateful. Did anyone tell you that I was almost kidnapped when I was very young?"

My gaze snaps down to hers. "No."

"I was a toddler, so I don't remember the incident. I'm told that the family was walking amongst the crowd for my father's birthday celebration. Shaking hands and saying hello, that sort of thing. All very normal."

For a royal, yes, I'm sure it is normal.

"I don't know how, but apparently, someone took my hand and pulled me into the crowd. It happened quickly, and with the bodies of people packed so tight, the security detail couldn't see me.

"It was a full-on panic. The rest of the family was immediately rushed back to the palace, but my father refused to go with them. He was absolutely determined to help look for me, which I'm sure only angered the guards."

"Without a doubt," I agree. "But he's a father, and I understand him wanting to get to you."

"Me, too. They found me less than ten minutes later, being carried to a vehicle only a few blocks away. A citizen saw me and started yelling, alerting the others."

"I hope they got a reward."

"He's my father's chef now," Ellie says with a bright smile. "Has been for twenty-three years. They became good friends."

The king is a good man. I've only spoken with him over the phone, and usually during times of stress, but he's been kind to me. Firm. Fair.

I respect him.

Suddenly, Ellie's phone dings, and she pulls it out of her purse to check it.

"What a bloody idiot," she mutters and shoves her phone back into the bag without replying. "In my experience, men are just horrible creatures."

Don't ask. Don't ask.

Do. Not. Ask.

"What's wrong?"

Why the fuck did I ask?

"That was Beauregard Hattenham. An absolute bore of a man with meaty hands. He asked me to marry him last week."

I stop walking and frown down at her. "*Marry* him?"

"As if I would," she mutters, still walking. "He doesn't love me. He doesn't even *like* me."

"Surely, he must if he asked you to marry him."

"He told me," she insists. "Said straight out that ours wouldn't be a love match, but with his *appropriate bloodlines*, we should get married. He's an earl. And if he wasn't such a jerk, it might have worked. But Beau likes to bully. He's mean. He sneers and judges and told me I'd need to have a boob job."

"What the fuck's wrong with your boobs?"

"Exactly," she says. "Not a thing. They may be on the smaller side, but I don't have a large frame."

"There's nothing wrong with your body," I grumble, ready to tear Beauregard Hatten*shit* apart.

"Thank you." She sighs, shaking her head. "But it's nothing new. The men I meet don't want *me.* They want the Crown. Alistair, a man I saw for over a year, insisted that if I'd just get pregnant, everything would be fine. The only thing *fine* in that scenario would be for Alistair's benefit. If I were pregnant, I would be forced to marry him, and he'd become a member of the royal family."

"Christ."

"There was no *way* I was going to sleep with him. He was slobbery and had sweaty hands."

She's met assholes. No wonder she's a virgin. I'm proud of her for not letting any of those morons touch her.

"It's exhausting," she admits as we wander down the path that leads to the bridge near Lauren's house. "Maybe I should just sleep with one of them and get it over with."

"No."

We walk to the top of the bridge, and Ellie leans against the side, looking down at the water.

"You don't want to sleep with those bozos."

She shrugs. "Perhaps joining a convent is the way to go."

I chuckle and turn her toward me, calling myself an absolute fool.

I can't believe I'm about to say this.

I must have a screw loose. I need therapy. A bullet to the head.

"I'll do it."

Her eyes widen in surprise. "You'll do what?"

"I'll be the one to show you the ropes when it comes to sex." I let myself touch her and brush a strand of hair off her cheek. "But we'll do it my way."

"I don't want you to agree because you pity me."

I sigh in frustration. Jesus, this woman would drive a saint to drink.

"I don't pity you." I take my hand away and watch as she swallows hard, listening carefully. "I like you. And, damn it, I'm attracted to you."

"I knew it," she whispers. "I knew it wasn't one-sided."

"There will be rules, though."

"Of course." She stands up straight and squares her shoulders.

"No one can know. And, no, it's not because I'm ashamed. I can't lose my job."

"Agreed. It's a secret. It's no one's business anyway."

"I'll teach you on my schedule, and my way."

"I'm the student." She nods and licks her lips. I see her skin has broken out in goose bumps.

"The rest, we'll make up as we go."

"That's reasonable."

I glance around, relieved when I see that we're alone. I know this is a stupid move. Someone could be hiding, taking photos.

But against my better judgement, I lean in, cornering her against the rail of the bridge.

I'm not touching her, but I can feel the warmth of her skin. Her breath comes faster, making her chest rise and fall with her heavy breathing. Her blue eyes are intent on mine as I lean closer, bringing my lips within an inch of hers.

Our breath mingles, and hers catches as her eyes drop to my lips.

It's a long moment of intense sexual tension so thick you could cut it with a knife.

"Lesson one," I murmur, "anticipation is everything."

And with that, I back away and walk down the bridge toward the car. When she doesn't follow, I turn to look at her.

"Are you coming?"

"Soon," she says as she finally moves her feet in my direction. "I'm hoping to very soon."

Holy hell, I'm an idiot for agreeing to this.

CHAPTER 4

~ELLIE~

"*A*nticipation is everything," I mutter, mimicking Liam from yesterday as I stare at myself in the mirror. I've brushed my long, blond hair at least six times. I can't get the memory of Liam and his hard body *almost* pressed to me on that bridge, his face so close to mine, out of my mind. I wanted him to kiss me more than I wanted my next breath.

In the privacy of my own home, I can admit that I almost grabbed his face and pulled him to me. Kissed him silly.

Well, I would have, if I'd known how.

Instead, I stood there like a ninny as he casually walked away from me as if nothing at all had happened.

My body hasn't stopped humming since, and he didn't even touch me.

"But he's going to," I remind myself with a wink. "He's going to *very* soon."

Because he gave me his word, and I don't think Liam's the kind of chap to go back on a promise.

Tonight, I'm in a light, breezy summer dress for dinner at Liam's cousin's house. I know I was only invited because I'm on Liam's detail, but I'm glad to go because I'm curious to meet his family.

I don't know why I'm so interested in my bodyguard, but I am. And for the next month, I can be as curious as I like.

I hear a knock as I step into my sandals.

I reach for my small Chanel handbag and open the door.

Liam's eyes immediately make a swift sweep over me, from top to bottom, and I feel my cheeks flush.

"It's just dinner," he says.

"I know."

"There's no need to wear a dress."

I smile, noticing that he's dressed down in a pair of cargo shorts and a simple black T-shirt.

"Dresses are all I have," I say as he leads me down the stairs.

"I've seen you in things other than dresses."

"When I'm home, I can wear what I like. But if I'm going out, it's a dress or a skirt. I've never gone out in anything else. It's expected."

He doesn't say anything for a moment as we walk

past the main house to where Liam's personal car is parked by the guest house. He opens the back door, but I shake my head.

"I can sit up front with you."

He glances my way. "You usually ride in the back."

"But this isn't the official car. It's *your* car. I'd like to sit with you."

He doesn't reply, just shuts the door, and then opens the passenger side. "Your Highness."

I sit and put on my seatbelt. Once he's settled in the driver's seat, I shift to look at him.

"What's wrong with you?"

His jaw is clenched, and his knuckles are white on the steering wheel. He's agitated.

Perhaps even angry.

"Nothing."

"Wrong answer. First of all, I'm Ellie, remember?"

He sighs.

"And you're angry. I've barely seen you today, so I'm not sure what in the world I could have done to make you cross."

He sighs again and then takes a deep breath, visibly relaxing.

"If it upsets you so much to bring me this evening, you should have said so."

"It's fine." He clears his throat. "It's not you, or dinner tonight. I'm sorry for being a dick."

"You're not a dick." My lips twitch at the word. "You can talk to me if you like."

He shakes his head. "I'm okay."

"So, we'll have sex, but we won't talk? Good to know."

He swiftly pulls to the side of the road. "I haven't decided when we'll have sex."

"But you said—"

"That we'd do it *my* way," he interrupts. He looks frustrated, his brown eyes on fire. "And, yes, we'll talk. But damn it, Ellie, this is new to me. I didn't ask for you to decide that we should give in to this chemistry. It's a bad idea. Every instinct is screaming at me that this is the worst idea I've ever had."

"I'm flattered." I'm hurt. He doesn't *have* to do anything. Including me.

"Jesus." He rubs the bridge of his nose. "I warned you that I'm not a nice person."

"You can take me home if having me with you is such a trial."

He shakes his head again, watches the traffic pass by, and finally reaches over and takes my hand in his, surprising me.

"I had a bad day."

"I'm sorry that you had a bad day."

I wait. I don't know him very well yet, but I have a feeling that Liam's the kind of person who will tell me what's on his mind when he's good and ready. His gesture of taking my hand is sweet, the touch comforting.

"A man I knew from the Army died this morning."

"Oh, I'm so sorry, Liam. You have my deepest condolences."

He nods. "He was only thirty-four. A good soldier. A nice guy."

I swallow and bring his hand up. His skin is warm and smooth against my lips.

"Was he in an accident?"

"No." He pulls away. I can feel the wall settling back into place, just like that. "He killed himself. He couldn't stand the nightmares anymore."

I gasp, watching Liam closely. "My God, Liam."

"Yeah, well. He wasn't the first. He probably won't be the last. But I shouldn't take it out on you."

"I'm sure Lauren wouldn't mind if we reschedule dinner."

"I'd like to go." He puts his car back in gear. "If you still want to go."

"Of course."

He nods and pulls back onto the street, passing the park where we walked yesterday and then pulls into a long driveway.

The house is large, and I live in some big homes. It's white with columns on the front porch and black shutters flanking each window.

"It's a lovely home."

Liam nods, looking at it. "My grandfather built it."

"Really?"

"Our great-grandparents helped to establish

Cunningham Falls. This property has been in the family for three generations now. I used to spend summers here when I was a kid."

"It looks like it was a fun place to be."

"We loved it."

He climbs out of the car, opens my door, and leads me up the steps of the porch. Before he can ring the bell, a little girl with red hair and a happy, toothless smile flings open the door.

"Liam!" she exclaims. "Mom! Liam's here."

"Who are you?" Liam demands as the little one flings herself into his arms. He holds her up high and buries his face in her neck, blowing raspberries. "I don't know you. You're too big."

"I'm Layla." She giggles with delight.

"Hi," Lauren says as she hurries to the door, a crying toddler in her arms. "I planned to be way more proper when you arrived, but Asa just fell, and Ty had to take a call, and well…here we are."

"I'm Ellie," I say, completely charmed by Liam's pretty cousin. It's not at all what I'm used to when meeting new people, and it's a complete breath of fresh air. "What can I do to help?"

"Come see my princess room," Layla says. "Please? Mommy said you're a *real* princess."

"I am," I reply as Liam lowers Layla to her feet.

"My God, what are we doing on the front porch?" Lauren says. "See? I'm a mess. Come inside."

She steps back and ushers us into a grand foyer with its large table full of fresh flowers.

"You have a lovely home."

"Thank you," Lauren replies. Asa watches me with big, tear-filled eyes.

"Sorry," a man says as he hurries into the room. "There's always a fire to put out somewhere."

He shakes Liam's hand.

"This is Pr—" Liam begins, but I shake my head.

"I'm Ellie," I say with a smile. Ty holds out his hand to shake mine, taking me off guard. But he doesn't know protocol. I take his hand and shake it. "It's a pleasure to meet you."

"We're happy to have you. Come on in. We're pretty casual around here."

"Ty's about to put the steaks on the grill. How do you take yours, Ellie?"

"Oh, medium, please."

I frown as we walk through the house to the kitchen that's open to the living space.

I don't know why it surprises me that they don't have a chef. Sebastian and Nina don't keep a chef on staff.

Most people don't.

Suddenly, I discover that Liam was right. I'm overdressed for the occasion, as everyone else is in casual summer clothes, and I'm wearing a dress appropriate for a summer garden party.

"Mommy, can I please show Ellie my room?" Layla asks with pleading eyes.

"Sweetheart, let's give Ellie a few minutes, okay?"

"I don't mind," I offer. It's true. Layla is adorable. "I have a niece and a nephew. I like children."

"Come on!" Layla takes my hand and pulls me up the stairs to her bedroom. It's a big space with an en suite bath. The child wasn't lying.

Her bed is shaped like Cinderella's coach with flowy, white curtains hanging from the canopy. There's plenty of pink in here, but the colors are muted and soft.

"This is a beautiful room, indeed. I can see why you love it so much."

"Does your room look like this?" she asks.

"Well, it was similar to this when I was a little girl," I admit. "Are those paper dolls?"

"Yeah, my aunt Jillian got them for me for my birthday."

I sit on the floor next to Layla, and we get lost in the world of make-believe and paper fashions.

"I LIKE THEM."

It's dark now, and we're driving back to Sebastian's house. We spent hours with Lauren and Ty and the girls, chatting and laughing. Eating delicious food. Watching the children and their antics.

"I do, too."

"Did you see when Asa just climbed right up in my lap?"

"The kids took a shine to you," he says with a smile. "In fact, I'd say they all did."

"Well, the feeling is mutual. It's nice to meet new people and make new friends. Lauren invited me to lunch, and she's an author, Liam."

"I know." He smiles over at me.

"I *love* to read. She gave me this to start with." I run my hands over the pretty book in my lap. "I'll start it straight away."

He parks his car and escorts me down to the boathouse.

I'm hoping, with all my might, that tonight is the night. Because he's been nearby all evening, and I've had perpetual goose flesh. I want him to touch me and do things to me that I can't even imagine yet.

"Would you like to come up?"

He pauses at the door, and just when I think he's going to say no, he nods. "For a bit."

Hello, butterflies. These are new. I'm rarely nervous around people, and certainly not around men.

But Liam is no ordinary man. He's handsome and mysterious. And even though he laughed and was perfectly fine all evening, I could see the little bit of sadness still in his eyes.

I drop my bag on the kitchen table along with my

new book and walk to the refrigerator. "Would you like something to drink?"

"No. Thanks."

I fill a glass with water for myself. My stomach still can't stand the idea of wine. But I need something for my suddenly dry throat.

I sit on the couch, expecting Liam to sit next to me, but he takes the chair instead.

"Thank you for allowing me to join you this evening."

He's watching me, his hands still on the arms of the chair.

Liam's the most intense man I've ever met.

And my father is a king.

"What are you thinking?" I ask.

Liam's lips twitch. He leans forward. "What are you thinking?"

"I'm wondering why you're not sitting on this sofa with me."

He licks his lips and then stands. With his eyes on mine, he slowly walks across the few feet that separate us. He doesn't sit next to me. No, that would be too easy. Too *ordinary*.

And Liam is anything but ordinary.

This man takes a knee in front of me and reaches out to gently tuck a piece of hair behind my ear. His brown eyes are hot, traveling over my face. When they land on my lips, he takes a shallow breath and licks his own, making me long for him more.

His fingertips travel lightly over my skin, down to my collarbone, and then he cups my cheek in one hand and leans in to kiss me.

It's over before it begins.

A peck on the mouth, and nothing more.

"I should go," he says.

"Are you playing games with me?" I blurt.

He frowns. "No."

"Liam, this is ridiculous. I'm not fifteen. I'm a woman, and you're treating me like—"

"Like what, Ellie?" He leans in again, his eyes on mine. "How exactly would you like me to treat you?"

"You know what I want," I whisper.

"And we'll get there. But I'm not going to carry you into that bedroom, strip you bare, and fuck you into the mattress. You're worth a hell of a lot more than that."

I blink rapidly, distraught at the thought of crying in front of him.

"Don't turn on the tears."

"I'm not." I shake my head. "I won't feel ashamed for wanting you."

"I'm not shaming you." His hand is gentle as he cups my cheek again. "And I'm not trying to treat you like a child. I'm trying to pace myself because I *want* to fuck you into the mattress."

"You do?" I sound ridiculously hopeful, even to my own ears.

He smiles, a rare expression that would knock a

woman on her bum from ten paces. "I'll be fighting the urge to come in here and do exactly that all night. But we'll get there. Anticipation, remember?"

"I hate your bloody anticipation."

"That makes two of us." He kisses my forehead and then my lips again before he stands. "I'll see you tomorrow."

"Okay."

He heads to the stairs.

"Liam?"

"Yeah?" He turns back expectantly.

"You know the code to the door. If you ever want to—"

"You're killing me, Princess," he mutters as he keeps walking to the door. "Goodnight."

"Goodnight."

I'm all smiles now, despite the sexual tension humming along every nerve ending. He wants me. He's trying to be chivalrous.

"You're leaving me?"

Nina laughs as she passes me a can of Coke from her fridge. I came over to the main house to have lunch with my brother and sister-in-law.

"Only for a couple of weeks," Sebastian says. "We'll be back soon."

"Where are you going?"

"Africa," Nina says. "I'm nervous. It's my first time."

"Oh, it's lovely. You'll enjoy it."

I glance out the windows and see one of the patrol boats making its way to the dock.

"You know," Nina says, "I'm surprised we haven't had more paparazzi around. Especially with you here, Ellie."

"No one knows I'm here," I say and shrug. "Except the family. I've kept it pretty low-key. And I'm not expected at any functions until the state dinner next month."

"We'll be taking Charles and Nick with us," Sebastian says. "That leaves just Liam and the ancillary staff for security here."

"I'll be *fine.* Honest. Absolutely *no one* knows I'm here."

"Yet," Nina says. "Because, eventually, someone will snap a picture of you and post it on social media."

"I'll stay close to home. I *love* it here. I'll also stick close to Liam."

In more ways than you know.

"See that you do," Sebastian says, always the protective big brother.

"I won't be naughty," I say, lying through my teeth. "I hope you have fun in Africa."

"Enjoy your downtime," Nina says. "I'm sure the girls will check in on you so you won't be lonely."

"I'll be fine. Wait. Will I have to cook for myself?"

Sebastian and Nina share a look. "Well, we can hire a chef to bring in your dinners if you want," Nina says.

"All I need is groceries," I tell them. "I can cook."

"Since when?" Sebastian wants to know.

"I've spent many hours with Chef at the palace, and I took some private classes. I can cook just fine, thank you."

"I didn't know that," Nina says. "We can certainly have groceries delivered. That's not a problem."

"Then it looks like I won't die of starvation, I have this beautiful place to spend time in, and I'm well protected. Thank you for thinking of me."

"We're glad you're here," Nina says. "Enjoy it. Everyone needs a true vacation once in a while."

"I plan to enjoy every minute of it," I inform them. "When do you leave?"

"This evening," Sebastian says.

"I'd better pack." Nina hops off her stool.

"We have people—"

"To do that for me, I know," Nina says, rolling her eyes. "But there are some things that I'd like to pick myself, thank you very much."

She kisses him as she walks past on her way to their bedroom suite.

"You could come with us," Sebastian offers.

"No."

"You always loved Africa."

"I do love it," I concede. "But I'm on holiday, and it's

quite lovely. But thank you for asking. You and Nina will enjoy it, and I'll see you in a couple of weeks."

"I'm worried about you."

"Why?"

"I don't even know why you're here," he says, and it occurs to me that I haven't explained what happened that made me come to Montana. So, I tell him the story. When I'm done, he's frowning.

"He thought he could bully his way into our family?"

"He did. And he was dead wrong."

"We really need to reinstate beheadings," Sebastian mumbles.

"That might be extreme."

"It's kind," he says. "Because I'd rather take him out and have him drawn and quartered. Beheading is too quick."

"He didn't rape me or anything."

Sebastian's eyes go ice-cold. "He would be dead if he had."

"I know."

He sighs. "You're really going to be okay here?"

"Yes. I'm not a baby anymore, you know."

"I know that. You're just not usually a solitary person. You prefer the company of others."

"Maybe that's been my problem. Perhaps I need to be here alone for a while, do some thinking, get reacquainted with myself. Or…for the first time, rather."

"Enjoy it." He hugs me close. "And let any of us know if you need anything."

"Thank you. I won't."

"Stubborn woman."

"Independent." I poke him in the ribs, making him wince. "I'm an independent woman."

"So you are. And a bully at that."

"You deserved it."

CHAPTER 5

Gunfire.

"Retreat! Retreat, goddamn it!"

They can't hear me. My men are sitting ducks in the middle of the street, being picked off by snipers one at a time.

"Adams!" I scream his name, but my second-in-command can't hear me. He looks around as if trying to find something, panic in his eyes. "I'm right here, damn it! Adams, get those men behind that building!"

He doesn't respond, doesn't follow my orders. Before my eyes, each of them dies, one by one until I'm the last one standing.

I run behind the building, and suddenly, there's Adams. He's talking fast.

"They've got snipers up on the top of the buildings," he says.

"I know. We can't get past them. It's going to be a

massacre."

"We've got more firepower," he insists. "We need to point up and keep firing until we get down the street."

"It's a suicide mission."

Didn't we just do this? What's happening?

"I'm scared," a private by the name of Beller says to the man next to him. "I have to tell my mom I love her."

"There's no time," Adams says. "We're going now. There's no time to waste."

"Don't go," I insist. "Do not *do this. You'll die. I'm telling you, you'll die."*

It's as though they can't hear me. Again. Why the fuck won't they listen?

They run away, and I hear the gunfire again. The screams. The cries.

I shoot up in bed, panting and dripping in sweat. The sheet is tangled around my legs. I barely free myself fast enough to hurry into the bathroom, where I heave until my stomach is empty.

I fucking hate the nightmares. Adams didn't die in that firefight when it happened.

But yesterday morning, he put the business end of a Sig Sauer P320 in his mouth and pulled the trigger. In the note, he said the nightmares were too much, the meds weren't helping, and he couldn't deal anymore.

He left behind a young wife and a two-year-old daughter.

"Fuck." I splash cold water on my face, rinse my mouth, and then stare at myself in the mirror. It's been almost ten years since that horrible day, and the night-mares have been less frequent. When I sleep, that is.

But Adams offing himself was a hard blow. It's been chewing at me since I received the call yesterday.

I need a run. The sun isn't up yet as I throw on some running gear, grab my bear spray, and jog down to the kitchen where my night shift guy, Aaron Reynolds, keeps watch on the perimeter cameras.

"Anything happening?" I ask.

"It's quiet. A couple of raccoons were on the driveway a while ago, but other than that, not much going on."

"Good. I'm going for a run. I won't be more than an hour."

Reynolds nods, and I take off through the back door and head down the path that connects to the trail system the city of Cunningham Falls laid about ten years ago. I'll go a short seven miles today, just enough to burn off some of this grief and energy.

Not to mention the sexual tension. Now that Charles and Nick are gone, accompanying Sebastian and Nina to Africa, I'm pretty isolated with Ellie. Which means I'll have an easier time of being with her.

But that's also bad because Ellie isn't the kind of woman that you fuck a few times and then go on your merry way. No, she's the type that sticks. I've always sworn that the sticking type isn't for me.

Yet I'll be damned if I can stay away from her. My blood runs thick when she's around, and my dick seems to have a mind of its own. She's just so damn beautiful.

And sweet. And everything good.

The pavement is even under my feet, the air brisk. Despite the heat during the day, Northwest Montana still cools off nicely once the sun goes down.

I push myself harder and faster, making my heart rate rise, and my breaths come quicker. The rush of blood in my ears drowns out the last of the gunfire from the nightmare. The sky starts to lighten from black to grey, and I decide it's time to turn back toward the house.

Cunningham Falls is sleepy this morning, with only a few vehicles out and about, manned by those going to work for the early shift. A paperboy rides his bike past me, tossing papers onto porches.

It makes me smile. In most of the modern world, people read the news on their phone or tablet. But here in this little town, a daily newspaper is still delivered.

I like it.

I'm dripping in sweat again as I slow my pace and head down the path to the house. Movement on the dock near the boathouse catches my attention, and I veer that way to check it out.

Ellie's sitting on the edge of the dock, her legs crossed, her eyes closed as she listens to the quiet.

I'm at once turned on by her and pissed that she's out here alone.

I'm not quiet as I approach, but she doesn't open her eyes.

"I could be an assassin."

"But you're not." Her lips tip up into a small smile. I want to cover her with my body, right here on the fucking dock, and take her immediately. She's so damn beautiful it takes my breath away, even when she's in her workout clothes with no makeup.

Especially with no makeup.

"But I could be," I repeat and prop my hands on my hips, still breathing hard. "I didn't know you were an early riser. I wouldn't have gone for a run."

She opens her eyes and looks up at me. "I didn't sleep much last night. I decided to come out here and watch the sunrise."

"With your eyes closed?"

"I was meditating."

"I have to go change," I say, looking back toward HQ and cursing myself for not taking my communication unit so I could call up for someone to come stand here. Reynolds should have seen her on the live feed.

"I'm fine." She smiles up at me innocently. "You can go change."

"I don't want you out here alone. I'll send Reynolds out until I can change."

"I can come with you," she offers.

If Ellie comes with me, I'll tumble her into my bed.

No. Bad idea.

"Can you just stay out of trouble for ten minutes?"

The smile remains in place. "Of course. I'm just sitting here waiting for the sunrise."

I nod and jog away. When I walk into the kitchen, I see red.

"Wake the fuck up."

Reynolds' head pops up. "What? Who?"

"You're fired."

"Ah, shit." He rubs his hands over his face. "I didn't mean to fall asleep. It wasn't more than five minutes."

"Long enough for Her Highness to walk out onto the dock and sit alone for God knows how long. She could have been shot, taken, *anything*. Because you weren't doing your fucking job. Now, collect your things and get the hell out of my headquarters."

"I don't deserve this," he mumbles as he fetches a lunch box out of the fridge and slams the door shut. "I'll sue for wrongful termination."

"I dare you to do just that," I reply calmly. "We don't employ anyone who doesn't take this job seriously, Aaron. I told you that when I hired you. You said you could handle it."

"Night shift has me all fucked up. Put me on the day shift."

"The low man on the totem pole always gets the night shift. And now you don't get that either. Go on."

He glares at me and then barrels out of the house, slamming the door behind him. I make a call to the two guys who were scheduled to come on duty in an hour, and they both agree to come in early.

Then I make one more call, clean up, and pull on clothes before jogging back out to the dock, where Ellie's still sitting as calmly as can be, staring up at the bright orange sky.

"It's so pretty here," she says without looking over at me. And I can admit, right here and now, I want her gorgeous blue eyes on me.

"I could have been an abductor."

She laughs and turns to look at me. "Sit."

"I'm officially on duty."

She shrugs a shoulder and pulls her knees up to her chest as she looks out over the lake again. "I just saw two bald eagles fly over the water. It was magical."

"There's a lot of wildlife here." I shove my hands into my pockets and skim the area with my gaze. It's calm and quiet. "We haven't had any issues with the press since you've been here."

"Only my family and a few close friends know I'm here," she says. "It should stay pretty quiet."

I'm grateful that she didn't make a big production about leaving England. It makes my job easier.

"I have a plan for today."

She glances up and arches a perfect eyebrow. "And what is that?"

"A breakfast picnic."

"A date?"

"A lesson," I correct her. "Lesson number two."

"What was yesterday?"

"That was an extension of lesson number one."

She laughs and then pushes herself gracefully to her feet. "Well, if frustration is lesson number one, I've mastered that. What do I need to wear for number two?"

"Casual. Pants, if you have them."

"I'll find something. We won't be going out in public?"

"No."

She nods and walks up into her apartment to change. Baxter and Bartlett arrive, and I brief them about firing Reynolds.

"I'll find someone else soon. In the meantime, we'll all be pulling a few extra shifts."

"Not a problem," Baxter says. "My wife wants to go to Hawaii for Christmas, so I'm saving up. I'll take some shifts."

"Thanks. I'll block the time off on the calendar for you during the holidays."

"Appreciate it," the other man replies, and then they walk to the house to get settled in for the day and relieve the remaining night shift man.

I keep two men on property guard duty at all times. One stays in the house to monitor the cameras, and one walks the perimeter on foot. They switch off and on throughout the day. If we have more royals visiting, I can pull in police officers who aren't on duty for extra help. Brad Hull, the chief of police, has been a valuable ally where the royals are concerned.

While Sebastian and Nina are gone, with Charles

and Nick in tow, it's just me and two other guards here at any given time. As long as Ellie keeps a low profile, that should be enough.

"Liam?"

I turn at the sound of my name and see Baxter escorting Aspen Calhoun, the new owner of Drips & Sips, down to the dock.

"She's good," I say to him and offer the woman a smile. "Thanks for doing this. I would have brought her to the coffee shop, but she's trying to keep her time here on the down-low."

"Oh, it's my pleasure," she says and passes over a basket. "There is coffee in there, along with some breakfast goodies."

"It smells damn good. I have cash—"

"I'm running you a tab," she says with a shake of her head. "Just square up with me the next time you stop in."

"I will. Thanks again."

"Aspen," Ellie says as she steps outside. She's in a cute pair of red shorts with a denim top tied in the front. Her long, blond hair is up in a ponytail, and her makeup is simple but perfect.

She looks so damn young.

Compared to me, she *is* young. Which is another reason why this is a bad idea.

"Hey," Aspen says and flashes a wide smile. "I was just dropping off this basket of goodies. I have to run back to the shop. I'm shorthanded today. But, Ellie, I'd like to invite you to have dinner with Monica, Natasha, and me at my place this weekend. You remember the girls from the salon?"

"Of course. That would be lovely."

"I'll need to have someone do a security check on your home," I say to Aspen, ignoring Ellie's scowl. "It's protocol."

"Anytime," Aspen replies. "Dinner will be a lot of fun. Natasha makes the *best* margaritas."

"What can I bring?"

"Just yourself. We're going to have Mexican food and Natasha's famous frozen margaritas on my deck. I have a great view. You'll love it."

"Thank you for inviting me," Ellie says as Aspen waves and hurries away. Then she turns back.

"Liam has my number," Aspen adds. "Just text me later, and I'll send you the specifics."

Ellie waves at Aspen and then turns to me with a sweet smile. I want to kiss the hell out of her. And I will.

Soon.

"Come on." I nudge Ellie toward my car. "I have a specific place I want to take you."

"We're not having a picnic here?"

I lean in to whisper in her ear. "Too many prying eyes. I want privacy."

She smiles and happily climbs into my car. I set the basket in the backseat, then jump in, start the vehicle, and pull out of the gated driveway, headed away from town.

I drive about three or four miles then turn onto a dirt road that leads down to the lake.

"This is a state park, but not many people come down here, especially at this time of day." I park the car and lead Ellie to a grassy area that overlooks the water, giving us a great view.

"Oh, it's pretty. Isn't it awesome how the view changes so drastically, but it's the same lake?"

"It's a big lake."

I spread out a blanket, and we sit next to each other.

"Coffee?" I say with a smile, pulling out a thermos and two Drips & Sips coffee mugs. "There's cream and sugar in here, too."

"I'll take all of it," Ellie says. "Do I smell scones?"

"Looks like huckleberry, still warm from the oven."

"Mine," she says, holding out her hand.

"Yes, ma'am." I pass her a scone, grab one for myself, and take a bite. "Damn, Aspen makes good scones."

"Mm-hmm." She chews, devouring the thing.

"Why couldn't you sleep last night?" I ask.

Ellie frowns, takes a sip of coffee to wash down the bite of scone, and shrugs a shoulder. "I guess I have a lot on my mind."

"Like what?"

I've often wondered what can be so stressful for royalty. I know they have responsibilities, but they live a life of privilege. What could be so concerning?

"Well, one of the charities I work with is for a children's hospital in London. I visit monthly to look in on patients. One of the little boys who has been there for many months was very ill the last time I visited a few weeks ago. I was thinking of him. He's lovely.

"I have several projects in the works for a facility for injured veterans who need both psychological and physical help, no matter their age in the UK. So, not just retired veterans. There needs to be much more outreach in that area."

I've stopped eating and am just staring at her as she talks about the things that she's passionate about. Her eyes are animated, her cheeks flushed as she gushes about her plans.

Ellie works her ass off. She's not just an indulged princess. She wants to make a difference in her country, and it makes me like her even more.

"Well, I'd say you're right. You do have a lot on your mind."

"I've already sent emails this morning to check in on everything and get status updates. I know I'm out of the country, but I want to be kept abreast of the situation there. That doesn't even include the conservation projects we have underway with endangered animals in Africa and Australia. I could bore you all day."

"You're not boring me at all," I reply and find myself rubbing the back of my finger up and down her bare arm. "I like your voice."

"Father tells me I talk too much," she says. "I think

it's because I have so many older siblings. I had to talk frequently and loudly to be heard. Do you have any brothers or sisters?"

I feel the smile fall from my face. "I had a sister. Belle was younger than me."

"Oh, no." She scoots closer and cups my cheek in her hand, throwing me off-kilter with her gentle touch. "What happened?"

"She drowned," I reply. "Here, in Whitetail Lake. I was sixteen, and she was about seven. We'd gone out on Lauren's parents' boat, and she jumped in to swim. She wasn't a good swimmer and was trying to show off. She hit her head, and I couldn't get to her fast enough to pull her out."

"And then last summer, I decided to be an idiot and take off on a boat," she says softly. "Now I know why you were so cross with me."

"It scared the shit out of me," I admit, my voice quiet. "It was that day all over again. I'm not afraid of the water. I can swim well, and boats don't bother me. But not knowing where you were that day was my worst nightmare happening all over again."

"I'm sorry," she says again. "And I'm so very sorry about Belle."

"She was a great kid. You would have liked her."

"If she was anything like you, I know I would have liked her very much," she says.

"Okay, enough sad talk." I set the picnic basket to

the side and turn to face Ellie. "Let's get on with your lesson."

"I'm a willing student. What is today's lesson?"

She's eager. And if the way she bites her lip is any indication, she's a little nervous.

"Let's recap what we know."

"You're killing me," she mutters, making me chuckle.

I drag my fingers through her thick hair and brush it to her back, exposing her shoulder. Her denim top is sleeveless, so I gently slide my fingertips over the ball of her upper arm.

Just that simple touch is enough to set me on edge.

As my hand slides down her biceps, I lean in closer and press soft, light kisses to her jawline and up to her ear.

"You're absolutely beautiful with the morning light flirting with your skin," I breathe. Ellie inhales sharply, and I drag my lips down her neck to her collarbone, then back up to her chin. "You make me want things, Ellie."

"Sexy things?" Her voice is shaky.

"Plenty of sexy things," I confirm. I know she wants me to kiss her. She's licked those luscious lips of hers twice. And she's going to get it, but I want to build the anticipation a bit more.

It appears I'm a masochist.

I urge Ellie onto her back and lean over her, one hand braced on the blanket by her head, the other still making lazy circles on the bare skin of her arm and shoulder.

She plants her hands on my sides, fists my shirt, and moans when I lay wet kisses on her neck.

"Oh, that's nice," she whispers.

"I think we've mastered the first lesson." I brush my nose across hers. "Now, lesson two."

With my eyes open, I lay my lips over hers. Softly at first. But when those hands of hers fist even harder on my sides, I can't help but give in to the kiss I've been dreaming about for a year.

I lick her lips, urging them open, and then I sink into her. I alternate between nibbling on her lips and exploring her mouth with my tongue. I let my hand roam from her arm to her side, and then cup her small breast over her shirt. I don't want to startle her.

But she's not alarmed at all. She arches into my touch, coming alive beneath me.

Jesus God, she's fucking incredible.

CHAPTER 6

~ELLIE~

So, *this* is what it feels like to be kissed silly. I've daydreamed about it for years. I've even had a few men try, but it was never right.

They were never right.

"You're thinking too hard," Liam whispers against my lips and then gets back to the serious business of kissing me like his very life depends on it.

He's kissing me because he's attracted to me, not just because of my lineage. My body doesn't seem to be my own as I writhe beneath him, silently urging him for more. What *more* entails, I'm not exactly sure, but I know I want it.

I push my hands under his shirt and feel the warm, smooth skin of his sides. He groans against my lips, which gives me courage. I let my fingers wander into his pants, cupping his bare bottom under his clothes.

"That's another lesson for another day," he mutters

and clenches his eyes closed. "Fucking hell, I love your hands."

I smile and give him a squeeze. "We can combine the lessons."

His hand glides from my breast, where my nipple is almost painfully hard, and moves down to my hip. My shirt has ridden up, and his thumb brushes light circles over my sensitive skin.

My entire body is on fire from these amazing new sensations.

If merely being kissed and touched feels this good, I can't even imagine how sex will be with this man.

His lips roam down my jawline to my neck. I can't stop the gasp that comes when he grazes a sensitive patch of skin. And then he pulls back and smiles down at me.

"You have a dimple right here." I brush my fingertip over the dent in his cheek. "You don't smile enough for me to admire it properly."

"Is that so?"

"It is. You've a handsome smile. You should show it more often. You're quite grumpy."

"I'm just serious about my job," he replies. "The head of security detail shouldn't be seen walking around with a goofy grin on his face."

"I suppose that would be inappropriate." I push up to brush my lips over the dimple in his cheek. "Just smile more when we're alone then."

"I'll try to remember."

"How old were you when you lost your virginity?"

He frowns and sits back, allowing me to sit up and straighten my clothes.

"That's a personal question."

"You'll know the answer to when I lost *my* virginity before long." I shrug a shoulder. "I'm curious."

"I was sixteen," he says but doesn't elaborate.

"And how old are you now?"

He glances over and narrows his eyes on me. "Thirty-five."

I nod slowly. "So, you have nearly twenty years of experience in this arena."

"I guess so."

I pick at the blanket beside my knee, trying not to be intimidated by Liam's vast sexual experience and my lack thereof. It's silly to be insecure.

"Your brain is going way too fast over there."

"I haven't the slightest idea what you mean."

"Right." He laughs and pulls me into his lap. His thumb tugs at my lower lip, and I hope with all my might that he'll kiss me again. "What's up, Princess?"

"I'm fine."

He leans in and presses his magical lips against my ear. "Tell me why you suddenly went cold on me, or I'll spank your royal ass."

I jump back with a gasp of surprise. "I beg your pardon?"

"You heard me." He brushes his nose over mine. The move melts me. "What's wrong?"

79

"You've a lot of experience."

"Yes, I have some. But I'm not super easy or anything."

His lips twitch, and I know he's trying to lighten the mood.

"I'm just a silly girl compared to you."

"You're not a girl," he replies, all humor gone from his eyes. "Your body, your mind, they are all woman. And you're in control here, don't forget that. If you're uncomfortable, or if you want to stop, all you have to do is say so. Every minute of every day."

"I don't want to stop. I'm not uncomfortable. I don't know why I'm suddenly concerned at all."

"I told you, I'm older than you. Ten years is a long time to gather additional life experience."

I nod. He's right, ten years is a long time. "It doesn't bother me, really."

"How do you feel?"

"Brilliant, actually." I lay my head on his shoulder. "This is nice. Quiet and secluded. I feel safe."

"You're always safe with me," he promises and kisses the top of my head. "We should probably get back. I have some reports to write up."

"Do you have a laptop?" I ask him.

"Yes."

"Why don't you bring it up to my apartment, and we can both work at the same time. You're supposed to be guarding me anyway."

"If I didn't know better, I'd say you're trying to find ways to see more of me."

I smile and climb off his lap. "I'm just encouraging you in your career of choice. And for now, that's me."

Liam chuckles and helps me gather our picnic things. Before long, we're pulling into Sebastian's driveway.

We walk down to my flat.

"You stay here," Liam says when we're safely in my kitchen. "I'm going to run to HQ and check in with the guys and grab my computer."

"I'm fine here," I reply with a smile. "Let yourself in when you return."

He nods and turns to leave, but then hurries back and kisses me right on the mouth. Not a soft peck like yesterday, but an intense, wet kiss that leaves my heart pounding as he smiles and then hurries down the stairs.

Liam is beyond sexy. I've never met anyone like him in my life. He's attractive, yes, and I'm ridiculously drawn to him.

But he's more than a pretty face. Or a fit body.

He's wonderful. Spending the next few weeks with him is going to be an absolute pleasure.

My phone pings with a text. I frown as I don't recognize the number.

The message is simple.

I know where you are.

I laugh and set my phone aside. "Sure, you do."

I don't know who *they* are, and the only ones who know where I am are those closest to me. People try and scare me all the time. They make false threats. Sometimes, someone gets ahold of my number and sends a preposterous message like this.

It's absolutely nothing. And I have more important things to think about.

I COULD SLEEP OUT HERE. The covered dock corner just off of the boathouse is officially my favorite place on the property.

It's shaded from the sun, and the furniture is soft and cozy. I sink into the cushions.

I've been reading Lauren's book today. Liam and I have had several fantastic days together. We worked side by side the other day after the kissing lesson. We watched a movie on the telly.

I'd like to coax him into Sebastian's small movie theater in the main house so perhaps I can have my way with him in the dark while the movie plays. I always saw that in films when I was young and thought it looked like fun.

But I haven't seen much of Liam today. I've been lazy, reading and dozing with the warm summer breeze floating over me. I haven't been this relaxed in ages.

Suddenly, Liam appears and kneels next to the couch, then leans in and kisses my nose.

"Napping?" he asks.

"Relaxing. I thought you wanted more privacy for this?"

"I was up at HQ, looking on the monitors, and I couldn't find you." His voice is calm, but there's a brightness to his brown eyes that I haven't seen before. An intensity. "So, I came to look. Didn't find you in your apartment."

"I'm not in my apartment. It's called a flat, by the way."

He leans in and kisses my lips. "And then I glanced over, and here you are, lying here, looking fresh and sexy as fuck."

Well, if that doesn't make a woman's core tighten, I don't know what will.

"That doesn't answer my question about affection here, where anyone can see."

"This pergola is on the monitors," he admits, "but this particular place is a blind spot."

"So that's why you didn't know where I was."

He nods slowly. "But I found you."

"And now that you have, what are you going to do with me?"

His eyes shoot down to my lips. His tongue flicks out to wet his own before he sinks his fingers into my hair and covers my mouth with his. Long and lazy, the kiss consumes me. Liam has a way with that mouth of his.

I want to pull him over me, feel the weight of him right here and now, but my phone interrupts us with a text.

I reach for it and frown at the same number from the other day.

Why aren't you answering me? I know where you are. Do you want me to prove it?

"Who the fuck is that?" Liam asks.

"I've no idea," I reply and move to set my phone down, but Liam takes it from my hands and scowls at the screen.

"This isn't the first text."

"No, but I don't recognize the number. It's probably some random weirdo who thinks it's funny to taunt me."

"You don't get to make that decision." He pulls back, quickly tapping on his own phone. "You give this shit to *me,* and I decide if it's worth worrying about, Ellie. Damn it, you *know better* than this. How could you be so careless? So damn stupid?"

I sit up and drop my head, feeling defeated. "I apologize."

"I'll take care of it from here."

His voice is cold. The playful, fun man from a few moments ago is gone.

"I'm headed to Aspen's house at four," I inform him

as I stand and walk toward my flat. "Please don't be late."

"Are all three of you from Cunningham Falls, then?"

We're sitting in Aspen's living room due to a storm that blew through and got the deck wet. The weather has cleared, but we decided to stay in where it's dry anyway. Aspen was right, she has a fantastic view of the mountains from her back yard. It's a lovely place.

Liam's sitting on the front porch.

I don't care one bit if he gets wet. I'm cross with him.

"Well, Natasha and I are," Monica says as she pours more salsa into a bowl. "We've been friends since we were small."

"I moved here about two years ago," Aspen adds. "I'm originally from Tennessee."

"That's rather far away," I say in surprise. "What brought you to Montana?"

"I was tired of being sad, and I wanted a fresh start," she says with a smile. "And that's all I'll say about that because we're having fun. This is not the time for sad stories."

"I'll drink to that," Natasha says and sips her margarita.

"Aspen was right," I say. "You make the best margaritas I've ever had."

"It's a secret recipe," she says and winks.

Natasha is stunning with long, curly, dark hair and brown eyes. She's tall and lean and looks as if she could be on the cover of a magazine.

Monica is just as beautiful but the exact opposite in features. With blond hair, blue eyes, and a figure that would make the Greek Gods weep, she's a stunner.

And don't even get me started on how gorgeous Aspen is. I've never seen red hair like hers before, and her green eyes are just so lovely.

"Ellie, I don't mean to be too forward, and I wouldn't say this if I was stone-cold sober—which I'm not because this is my third 'rita—but your bodyguard is kinda hot."

Aspen and Monica nod at Natasha's proclamation, and I scowl.

"On any normal day, I would agree with you. But I'm mad at him today."

"Why?" Aspen asks. "Did he come on to you?"

I chew on my mostly numb lip, wondering how much I should say. I don't know these women well. What if I tell them our secret and then they run off and tell the press?

"You don't have to tell us," Monica says. "Honest. It's none of our business anyway."

"It's not that he's been inappropriate," I say, choosing my words carefully. "I received a weird text a few days ago, and then another one today. I didn't recognize the number. Sometimes, if someone finds my digits somehow, they send me ridiculous messages. I usually just block them and get on with my life, no problem.

"But Liam saw today's message and got really angry with me because I didn't show it to him sooner. He called me *stupid.*"

I feel my cheeks heat at the thought of what he said.

"Well, that seems uncalled for," Aspen says and frowns. "I don't know Liam very well, or at all now that I think of it, but that seems harsh."

"You should tell him that he's not allowed to speak to you like that," Natasha says. "You're his boss, Ellie. You don't have to take that."

"It took me by such surprise, but you're right." I pull my phone out of my handbag and pull up Liam's number. "I'll text him."

"He's right outside," Aspen says with a snort. "Just go and tell him off."

"If I go out there, I'll just want to kiss him again." I slap my hand over my mouth and stare in shock at my three new friends.

"I *knew* it," Natasha says and pumps the air with her fist. "He looks at you like you're the most delicious thing he's ever seen."

"Well, I...he does?"

"Oh, yeah," Monica agrees. "I wish my husband looked at me like that."

"He does," Aspen says and rolls her eyes. "Rich is completely in love with you."

"We're talking about Ellie," Natasha reminds us. "And Monica and I *do* know Liam from when we were younger. He was friends with Monica's brother, Sam."

"They're still good friends," Monica says. "And Liam's a nice guy. A little tortured, I think, but super nice."

"He calls princesses *stupid*," I remind her. "And I'm gonna give him a piece of my mind."

I type vigorously on my phone and say the words aloud as I slowly type them.

"You were mean today. I'm not accustomed to allowing bullies to kiss me. In fact, I've avoided it like the plague. Consider this my resignation from our agreement."

"I want to know what the agreement was," Monica mutters and shoves a chip loaded with guac into her mouth.

I set the phone aside with a decisive nod. "There. That'll show him."

"Is he a good kisser?" Aspen asks.

"So bloody good," I admit with a sigh and take a drink. "Why does he have to be so good at that? And why do I want him to do…*things* to me?"

"Because he's a hot man," Natasha reminds me. "Of course, you want him to do things."

"What kinds of things?" Aspen asks, leaning in closer. "Give us details."

"Well, that's not really something—"

"None of our business," Monica reminds the room, but Aspen waves her off.

"Come on. I haven't had a man interested in me in way longer than I care to admit. Give us some details. This is girls' night, Ellie. We're in the vault."

"We won't tell a soul," Natasha says. "We take girl talk very seriously. And we're not the kind of women who try to hurt each other."

"They're right," Monica says. "We won't tell."

"I'm a virgin," I blurt and look down in humiliation. "I asked Liam to take care of that little detail. And he agreed. But he's been taking me through *lessons*, starting with anticipation and then kissing. We've only made it to the kissing part, and I have to admit, it's nice."

"First of all, being a virgin is nothing to be ashamed of," Aspen says and loops her arm around my shoulders. "And, second of all, that's an awesome plan."

"Hell, yes," Natasha agrees. "And it's pretty sweet that he's taking you through lessons rather than just getting the deed done and getting on with his life."

"But I just told him we're done with it all."

All three of them stare at me as if I just declared war on the United States.

"Why?" Aspen asks.

"Because he *yelled* at me today. And he was mean."

"Obviously, he must be punished," Monica says, tapping her lips with her finger. "But I wouldn't abandon the plan entirely. He *is* hot. And nice."

He's wonderful.

I'm mad at him, but I might have spoken too soon.

"Okay." I pick my phone back up. "I'll tell him never mind."

Sorry. I meant to send that text to someone else.

I smirk and set my phone aside and enjoy my evening with my new friends. Until I met Nina, I didn't know what it meant to *trust* friends. My acquaintances in London are snobby, elitist, and petty. They're certainly not the kind of women I'd want to confide in.

But the new friends I've made are so different.

Once all of the tacos, nachos, and margaritas are gone, I decide it's time to return home for a good night of sleep.

I hug the others—which is new for me, but lovely— and pull the front door open to find Liam standing on the other side. His jaw is tight. His eyes hard.

"I'm ready to go home."

He nods and escorts me to the car. We took the official car tonight, at my insistence. I didn't want to ride in the front seat with him.

The trip is quiet, the walk down to my flat silent.

Liam unlocks the door and helps me up the stairs. I'm not as drunk as that night at Brooke's Blooms, but I'm not exactly steady on my feet either.

"We need to talk," Liam says once we're up in my place.

"You yelled at me," I blurt. "And you called me *stupid*, Liam. I will not stand for that."

"I'm sorry." He sighs and rubs his hand over his face. "I apologize for saying that. It was wrong of me. You're *not* stupid at all. But, Ellie, you *have* to tell me about anything that isn't normal. I can't protect you if I don't know what's threatening you."

I sink down onto the couch and watch him pace my living room.

"My priority is making sure you're safe. It's my job, yes, but it's more than that. I care about you, damn it, and I'll do whatever I have to, to make sure you're protected. There are no exceptions, even if you think it's silly. You, your safety, is the most important thing."

I don't even stop to think twice, I just stand and launch myself into his arms. I wrap my legs around his waist and my arms around his neck and hold on tight.

"Apology accepted. And I'm sorry for not telling you. I won't do it again."

"Thank you." His hands are on my bum as he kisses my cheek. "Now, I have one more question."

"Okay."

"Who the fuck did you mean to send that text to?"

I frown and pull back so I can look him in the eyes. "What text?"

"The one you sent me when I was sitting on Aspen's wet porch."

"Oh." I bury my face in his neck again, enjoying his scent. "I really did mean to send it to you, but then I regretted it and sent the second one."

He carries me to the bedroom and sets me on the floor. "Sleep off this tequila, and I'll see you tomorrow."

"Stay." I catch his hand before he steps away. "Please, stay with me. We'll just sleep. Talk. I want you to hold me."

He seems to think it over, then rubs his lips together and nods. "Okay."

I clap my hands but then frown when he pulls my pajamas out of a drawer and holds them out for me.

"Go change in the bathroom."

"You've touched me pretty much everyw—"

"Go. Change," he says again. "Please."

I do as he asks. When I return to the bedroom, the linens are drawn back on the bed. Liam is wearing a T-shirt and shorts.

"Were you wearing that under your suit?" I ask.

He nods.

"You can take the shirt off if you want."

He shakes his head no.

"Can't you speak anymore?"

"You're so fucking beautiful, my head might explode."

His voice is rough, his hands fisted in the bed linens. I may be a little impaired, but I know that he wants me.

I also know that he'll be a perfect gentleman, damn him.

I walk to the bed and climb inside the sheets. When I wait expectantly, Liam joins me. I immediately scooch next to him and lay my head on his chest. His arm wraps around me. I can hear his heartbeat.

"This is nice."

"Mm-hmm."

"Your heart is beating fast."

"Yep."

"Are you tired?" I push my hand under his shirt and sigh when I feel the warm flesh of his hard stomach. "You have great skin."

"Okay." He rolls me over and snuggles me from behind. "You've forced me to spoon you. Keep your hands to yourself, Princess, or you'll ruin my whole plan."

"I like touching you."

He kisses my head and whispers, "Go to sleep, sweetheart."

CHAPTER 7

I've never woken up with a man in my bed before. Well, unless you counted the few times when I was sick as a child, and my father was there to comfort me. Though that was rare, as I usually had nannies to tend to me.

Waking up with Liam wrapped around me is a whole new experience. I fell asleep with him pressed to my backside, but now my head is on his chest, his arms holding me close, our legs tangled.

It's as if we've been lovers for years. Natural.

It feels bloody amazing.

"Good morning," he murmurs and kisses my head.

"It *is* rather good, isn't it?" I snuggle against him and smile. "Did you sleep well?"

"Surprisingly, yes." He sighs and shifts his legs, rubbing one up and down mine. I want to purr.

"You don't usually sleep well?"

"No."

"Why?"

"You're too full of questions for this time of day." He rolls me onto my back and smiles down at me. "Did you sleep?"

"Like a baby."

"I think"—he presses a sweet kiss to my cheek—"we should"—kisses my nose—"move on to"—another on my chin—"lesson three."

"Fantastic."

He pauses to kiss me on the mouth, one of his slow, deep kisses that make me weak in the knees. It's a good thing I'm lying down.

His hand travels from my hip, up my side over my shirt, and lands on my breast, where the nipple is already hard and waiting for him. He tweaks it, pulls on it, and then journeys to the other side to pay that breast the same attention.

"This lesson," he whispers, "is called *heavy petting* here in the States. I have no idea what you'd call it."

"Frustrating," I groan and arch into his touch. But then he surprises me by slipping that hand *under* my shirt, then up my stomach and back to my breasts. "Oh, that's better."

"So soft." He kisses down my neck and settles in to nibble on that most sensitive place.

"You give me the shivers."

"That means I'm doing something right."

He's pressed to my hip, and I can feel his hardness

there. I want to see it. Touch it. *Taste* it. There's so much I want to do with him, and he's going at this snail's pace that's absolutely driving me mad.

But it also feels so bloody good.

I join in the fun, pushing my hands under his shirt. I roam over his skin leisurely, soaking him in. I drag a foot up his bare leg.

I'm consumed by him and his sexiness.

When my hands wander around to his back, he takes them and pins them above my head with a firm grip, holding me with just one hand.

"Lower," I rasp as his fingers brush over my stomach.

"What do you want, sweetheart?"

"I want your hand *lower.*"

To my utter shock, he complies. But he doesn't dip under my pajama shorts. No, he stays over them and presses his hand against my center.

I've never felt anything like it. "*Liam.*"

"You're incredible," he rasps. "Look at me."

I open my eyes and find his gaze already on me. I can't help but arch up into his touch, longing for more. I can feel *something* happening, and I desperately want it. But just as I'm about to get there, Liam's phone rings loudly.

"Fuck," he murmurs, burying his face against my neck. "God, babe, I'm sorry."

I can't reply as he rolls over and fetches his phone.

"Cunningham," he barks into the device. His eyes

dart to me, and then he's hurrying from the bed and pulling on clothes. "When? Is Baxter headed there? Good. I'm with the princess now. I'll stay here until he reports in. Keep me posted."

He hangs up and pulls on his pants, cringing when he tucks in his cock and then zips up.

"What's happening?" I sit up and push my hair off my face.

"Apparently, there's been a security breach. The camera on the path that leads into the woods is out, and there was a man on that camera moments before."

He pulls a handgun out of a holster, shocking me. He checks the magazine, then pushes the weapon back into its cradle.

He glances my way. "Why do you look surprised?"

"I never see your weapon."

He loops his arms through the holster and secures it around him, then slips his jacket on over it.

"I'm always armed," he replies. His voice is cold now, his body tight, his face devoid of emotion.

"How do you turn it off so quickly?"

"Turn what off?" He's staring out the window now, his broad back to me.

"The emotions. We were having an incredibly intimate moment. I was about to explode beneath you, and thirty seconds later, you're just…"

"Just what?"

"Cold."

He turns and looks at me for a long moment.

97

"What I'm feeling for you is anything but cold. But this is my *job*, Ellie. Your life may be at risk. I was hired to protect you."

"It's fascinating," I admit with a sigh. "Watching you work, after having shared other things with you. It's interesting."

Liam's phone rings again. He has it answered and pressed to his ear before I can blink.

"Report."

He listens carefully, and then his body sags in relief. "Good. I was about to call Hull in for backup. Thanks, Baxter."

He hangs up and holsters his weapon.

"All clear?"

Liam nods. "It was a jogger, and he took the path by accident. Tripped on the camera. Baxter did a quick background check. He's clean."

"Good."

He walks to me and tips my chin up with his finger. "Are you okay?"

"I've been sexually frustrated my whole life." I shrug. "I'm fine."

"I'm sorry." He kisses my lips gently. "Next time, we won't be interrupted."

I nod, confident that what he says is true. Liam's not the type to offer hollow promises.

"I suspect you have to go to headquarters."

"I do." He takes a deep breath. "But I won't be too long."

An idea has been working its way through my head for a couple of days.

"Actually, take all the time you need. I'm going up to the main house for the day."

"I'll wait and escort you."

I hop out of bed, change my clothes, and rather than waste time showering and primping here, I gather the things I'll need.

I can do all that once I'm in the main house.

"I'm ready."

"THANKS FOR COMING on such short notice." I smile at Natasha and Monica, who are currently sitting in the living room, enjoying the view of the lake. "I'm sorry Aspen couldn't join us."

"She practically lives at the coffee shop," Natasha says. "It's her passion."

"I admit, it feels odd to talk about this with you both now that I'm sober."

"Oh, this is going to be good." Natasha leans in, ignoring Monica's rolling eyes. "What's up?"

"I want to go to the cinema with Liam."

Both of them just continue staring at me as if waiting for a punch line.

"We have a movie theater in town," Monica says at last.

"I *can't* go out to the movies," I reply. "I'm trying to stay relatively discreet."

"Well then, that rules out movies in the park," Natasha says.

"What is that? It sounds lovely."

"On Friday evenings during the summer, we have movies in the park," Monica replies. "They're usually films that have been out for a while, but it's a chance for people to go and hang out in the nice weather, doing something fun. Our summers are so short, we tend to try and enjoy every moment."

"As much as I would *love* that, I'm afraid it's out. And I'd like to do this today. There's a movie theater here in this house. I just want your ideas for things I should do for it. I've never been to a traditional theater to see a movie."

"You haven't?" they ask in unison, both taken aback.

"We have a theater in the palace," I say quietly. "And, sometimes, we're invited to premieres. I've been to a few of those, but I don't think they count as a normal cinema experience."

"Definitely not," Natasha says just as Monica's phone rings.

"Sorry, guys, it's my brother." She quickly answers. "I'm busy, what do you want? Uh-huh. Okay. Yeah, I can."

Natasha and I share an amused glance. Monica's face is so expressive.

"Right. Got it. I *got it.* I won't forget. Gotta go. Bye." She sighs and tucks her phone into her pocket. "Sorry."

"What's Sam up to?" Natasha asks, trying to sound nonchalant, but it's not working.

"I don't know," Monica says. "He wants me to take something somewhere. Oh! He needs me to take his boots to the fire station."

"He forgot his boots?" Natasha asks.

"Different boots. I don't ask a lot of questions," Monica says with a shrug.

"Is your brother a firefighter?" I ask.

"Yeah, he used to be an EMT, but he recently moved into a firefighter position. He's pretty badass. We're all proud of him."

"You should *see* him in his gear," Natasha adds, waggling her eyebrows. "Hello, hotness."

"Nat's had a crush on my brother since middle school," Monica says, waving her best friend off. "And, no, I don't look at him like that when he's in his gear because he's my *brother.* That's disgusting."

"Not from where I'm sitting," Natasha says with a smile. "But let's get back to the task at hand. Movies."

"Right." I nod and wring my hands. "I don't know why I'm so nervous."

"Me either," Monica says. "It doesn't take anything fancy. Just a dark room and a movie."

"Wrong," Natasha says. "She needs popcorn. Soda. Maybe some licorice."

"Let's go see what we're working with," Monica suggests.

"Good idea." I gesture for them to follow me and lead them downstairs to where the theater is located.

"It's like a lobby out here," Monica says in surprise. "You have plenty of candy, a soda machine, and a popcorn popper."

"We just have to make the popcorn," Natasha says with a nod. "We've totally got this. In fact, why don't you text Liam and ask him to come down here in thirty minutes? We'll serve your goodies, and then leave when you're settled to do...whatever you want to do in there."

"Really?" I'm stunned that they're so excited to help me. But I shouldn't be. Isn't this why I asked them to come over?

I know I've only recently met them, but I feel like I can trust them. I'll miss Montana and these wonderful women that I've come to know in such a short time when I leave.

I don't want to think about that now. I have a surprise to set up.

"We've totally got this," Natasha says. "It's so fun. Go primp or something and let us do this. Don't forget to text Liam."

"You're so wonderful. I'll be back in twenty," I promise and hurry up to the guest room where I stashed my things. Before long, I've styled my hair, done my makeup, and thrown on a simple sundress.

When I make my way back downstairs, the incredible smell of fresh popcorn greets me.

"Good afternoon, and welcome to Royal Cinemas," Natasha says with a smile. Before I can reply, Liam walks in behind me.

"What's all this?"

"The movies," Monica replies and winks. "We're showing Sherlock Holmes today. What can we get you to snack on?"

"Popcorn is a must," Natasha says, filling a big bucket with the kernels. "What else?"

"I'll take a Coke," I reply. "And some Junior Mints."

"Good choice," Monica says. "And you, sir?"

"Uh, I'll have a root beer. The popcorn is enough for me."

"There's plenty out here, and we offer free refills," Natasha adds. "But you'll have to get those yourself because we're about to leave."

"Have fun," Monica says as Liam and I walk into the theater.

I don't know how they managed it, but just as we sit down, the movie starts, and the lights dim.

"This is a surprise," Liam says as we sit smack dab in the middle of the room. He shoves a handful of popcorn into his mouth. "But a fun one."

I sip my Coke and suddenly feel nervous again. I wanted to do this, but now that I have Liam here, what am I going to do with him?

He's supposed to be teaching *me*.

I reach for some popcorn and smile when my hand brushes his. Before long, we're engrossed in the film, enjoying our snacks and each other.

About an hour in, Liam sets the empty bucket on the floor and takes my hand in his. He kisses my knuckles, my wrist, and then my shoulder.

I didn't realize the armrest between us was moveable, but he must have known because he lifts it and shifts closer to me.

"You're beautiful," he whispers in my ear.

"Thanks," I say.

"Shh." He nibbles my earlobe. "We're in the theater. We have to be quiet so we don't disturb anyone."

I start to laugh, but then he kisses my ear again and starts playing with my hair. I'm a goner.

All coherent thought dissipates from my mind, and all I can think about is this man and his magical mouth.

"Making out in a theater isn't a lesson that came to mind," he admits as his hand glides down to my breast. "But it's something everyone should experience at least once."

"I daydreamed about this," I admit with a whisper and then moan when his thumb pushes against my hardened nipple.

"We're going to discuss more of those daydreams."

And that's it. Something bold within me rears its head, and I boost myself up and straddle Liam's lap. My mouth crashes over his. Liam's hands are on my bum, and we take this make-out session to the next level.

I want to get naked. I want him to take me right here, on this seat.

But I know he won't.

That doesn't stop me from grinding down on him and relishing the powerful feeling that pours through me when I feel him harden.

"Fucking hell," he growls before fisting his hand in the back of my hair and pulling me down for more kisses.

He tugs my dress down in the front, exposing one naked breast, and wraps his lips around the nipple, sucking hard.

Oh, my God.

My head falls back, my center grinds down harder on him, and with his mouth tight on that sensitive bud, I feel something massive and *marvelous* move through me.

I cry out and shudder, and everything in me tightens.

I do believe I've just had my first orgasm.

Liam kisses my chest, my neck, and when he feels me start to loosen up, he pulls me down into his arms.

"Are you okay?" he asks.

"I don't know that I've ever been better," I confess. "Liam, I think I—"

"You did." His voice is confident, and he sounds quite pleased with himself. "You had one kind, anyway."

"There are different *kinds*?"

He laughs and kisses my forehead. "A few that I know of. Congratulations, sweetheart."

"This was a bloody good idea."

He laughs again, and I enjoy the sound of it. He doesn't laugh often enough.

"Agreed."

"I'M STILL NOT CONVINCED that this is the time or place. Couldn't you make your own coffee at home?" Liam asks as he parks his car in front of Drips & Sips.

"My coffee isn't as good," I reply. "Liam, it's two o'clock on a Wednesday. I don't think the place is going to be packed to the gills with people just waiting to get a peek at me, should I happen to be in town."

"You don't know that."

I roll my eyes and move to get out of the car, but he stops me with a hand on my arm. "Wait. I'll come around."

I do as I'm told, and Liam and I walk into the coffee shop together. It smells delicious. I love that it's also a gift shop, and take a moment to admire the array of fun things that Aspen has for sale.

I'll have to remember to come back and gather some gifts for my family before I return back to London.

"Well, this is a fun surprise."

I look over at the sound of Aspen's voice and offer

her a friendly smile. "I thought it would be fun to drop in and see how you are. I hope that's okay."

"You're welcome here anytime, Ellie. I'm glad you came. Can I make you something?"

"A chai latte would be lovely."

I follow Aspen to the counter and watch as she fusses with my drink. "Have you had a busy day?"

"Every morning is busy, and thank goodness for it," she says with a wink. "But afternoons usually slow down a bit. We close at four, so this is the perfect time to stop by."

"I'll remember that." I accept the drink and take a sip. "This is delicious. How much do I owe you?"

"That's on the house."

"You don't have to do that."

"It's your first one," she says, waving me off. "Hopefully, you'll be back for more."

"You can count on it." I glance to my right and smile. "I'm going to go say hello to someone."

"Enjoy," Aspen says.

"Did you see that Lauren's here?" I ask Liam, who's been quite silent since we arrived.

"Of course, I saw her."

"You didn't go and say hello."

"I'm working with you," he reminds me as we walk to Lauren's table.

"Hey, you two," Lauren says with a smile. "I just finished writing a chapter."

"I didn't know you wrote here. Don't you have an

office at your home?" I ask.

"Sure, but sometimes, I need a change of scenery. If I do, I usually come in here. What are you two up to?"

"I talked Liam into bringing me into town for something to drink, and a change of scenery of my own."

I reach out to put my hand on Liam's arm, but he backs away from me. I blink rapidly, trying to keep up with my conversation with Lauren.

"Oh, here's Sam," Lauren says. "Sam, have you met Princess Eleanor?"

"Can't say I have."

I turn to see a tall man with broad shoulders and strawberry blond hair. His smile is friendly as he nods.

"Ellie, this is Sam Waters."

"It's nice to meet you."

"It's a pleasure to meet you, as well. I've heard a bit about you from your sister. Monica says you recently joined the fire department?"

"That's right. Hey, Liam, can I talk to you for a second?"

"Sure." Liam turns to me, and still without touching me, says, "Stay right here. I'll be within eyesight."

The two men walk away to the other side of the coffee shop and immediately delve into conversation.

"Are you okay, Ellie?" Lauren asks.

I'm confused. Hurt. Perhaps disappointed.

But I paste a smile onto my face and nod. "Oh, yes, I'm just fine, thank you."

CHAPTER 8

"*I* haven't seen you since you moved home, and it's been a year," Sam says.

"Time flies fucking fast." I rub my hand over the back of my neck. "At least I text."

Despite not living here full time, Sam was always one of my closest friends growing up. We kept in touch when I was back in Washington, and we were practically inseparable when I was in town for the summer.

There are few men that I trust more than Sam Waters.

"She looks like a handful. A beautiful one, I might add."

I glance Ellie's way and smile. She's talking with Lauren, her hands as expressive as her gorgeous face.

"She's both," I agree. "I heard you're doing firefighter work now. Good for you, man."

"I liked being an EMT. But I enjoy this more.

Speaking of, you should come out with some of us tomorrow night. We're just going to shoot pool for a bit, but you'd enjoy it. Have a beer or two and shoot the shit with the guys."

As good as the idea of spending time with my best friend sounds, I start to shake my head.

"Unless you've lost your touch when it comes to pool." He rocks back on his heels. "We wouldn't want to embarrass you or anything."

"I'd kick your ugly ass." It's a good-natured snarl that makes Sam laugh.

"What's so funny?" Ellie asks when she joins us. She stands closer to Sam than to me, as if she's putting space between us on purpose. I narrow my eyes at her.

"I was just ribbing Liam and criticizing his pool-shooting skills," Sam says. "Or lack thereof."

"I haven't lost my pool-playing abilities," I reply calmly. "I just don't have to prove it to you to be confident in myself."

"So, come out with us tomorrow night and prove me wrong."

"I can't—"

Ellie cuts me off. "Going out would be wonderful. He could use a night away from work. Count him in."

I lift a brow. Sam's smile deepens.

"Awesome. I'll text you tomorrow." He nods at Ellie. "Nice to meet you."

Sam walks out of Drips & Sips, and I turn to Ellie.

"Last time I checked, you didn't make my schedule."

She doesn't reply. She simply walks out of the shop with her head held high and her shoulders back, stopping by the car and waiting for me to open the door for her—which I do.

The ride to the house is full of silence. She's clearly pissed off about something, but I'll be damned if I know what. So, I let her brood with her arms crossed and her nose pointed at the passenger window.

I walk her down to the boathouse and reach for her hand when we're inside her apartment, but she jerks away and scowls up at me.

Here we go. I'm about to get it. I'm not sure exactly why I'm about to be in trouble, but I brace myself for Ellie's temper.

"Oh, so *now* you want to touch me?"

I frown. "What does that even mean?"

She shakes her head and moves to stomp away, but I catch her elbow and turn her back to me.

She looks down at my hand and then back up at my face and says with ice in her voice, "Take your hand off me."

"You won't run from me," I reply, but drop my hand as she asked. "If there's a problem, you'll tell me right here and now what it is. I don't have time for childish games."

"*Childish games?*" She rounds on me, boosting up to her full height as she jabs her finger in my chest. "I'm not the one playing *childish games*, Liam Cunningham. That would be *you*. And I don't have time for that either. So, you can go about your business, and I'll do the same. I'll ring for you if I need you."

"No."

She levels me with that regal princess look she has. "Excuse me?"

"I know you're not used to being told no, but *no*. What's got you so damn pissed off?"

"You recoiled from my touch not thirty minutes ago."

"When?"

She stares at me as if I'm stupid and crosses her arms over her chest. "At the café," she replies. "I went to touch your arm, and you backed away as if being touched by me was repulsive."

I sigh and run my hand down my face. "Your touch is not repulsive."

"You made me feel as if it is." She sniffs, her nose in the air as if she can't be bothered with me anymore. But her blue eyes hold the hurt she won't admit to aloud.

"I didn't mean to hurt your feelings."

"Don't flatter yourself. It would take a lot more than that to hurt me."

She turns away, but I reach for her again. She doesn't pull away this time.

"I was on duty," I remind her and drag my fingertip down her smooth, pale cheek. "And not only that, but we were also in public."

She blinks rapidly as if she'd forgotten. I have to remember that she's young *and* inexperienced.

"Someone could have snapped a picture and posted it all over social media, then your cover would have been blown," I continue. I press a light kiss to her forehead. "You know that better than anyone."

"I'm daft," she whispers.

"No, you're not. You're a woman in an intimate relationship with a man. Casually touching me isn't inappropriate most of the time, but we have to remember that this isn't a normal situation. It's my job to protect you, and that includes making sure you're never in a position that puts you at risk."

"I know you're excellent at your job," she says. "And I understand that what we do behind closed doors is ours alone. I'll be more mindful when it's not just the two of us."

"If this is blurring too many lines for you, making it difficult, we can end it."

Say you don't want to end it. The thought of not touching her anymore makes me crazy. I haven't even been inside her yet, and I'm already addicted to her. I've never felt this way before. If a woman decided it wasn't working for her, I didn't care if she moved on.

I'm not ready to say goodbye to this relationship with Ellie.

"No." She sighs. "I lost my mind there for a moment, but I'm fine now, thank you."

I kiss her forehead again, and when she tips her face

up, I brush my lips across hers. I can't get enough of her taste. Taking things slow is a torturous, painful mini-death but I'm also enjoying the task of introducing Ellie to her sensuality.

Losing one's virginity doesn't have to be a wham-bam-thank-you-ma'am. She should be seduced, slowly.

I might be a dead man when all is said and done, but it'll be worth it.

I slip my hands up her arms and cradle her face as I sink into her, kissing her long and slow. She always moans softly, surrenders herself completely to me.

It's a damn sight to behold.

But rather than letting me take things further, she plants her hands on my chest and backs away a few inches, far enough that my lips can't reach her.

I want to growl and yank her against me, but I wait to see what her next move is instead.

"I don't have time for this." She's breathless. "I have work to do today."

"Later, then." I brush my nose against hers. "We'll make up for our argument later."

"Epic mail day," Baxter says the next morning as he sets a plastic tote brimming with boxes and letters on the table. Each day, I meticulously go through the mail before delivering it to the royals.

It's protocol.

"I'm headed out to check the perimeter," the other man says before walking out and shutting the door behind him.

There are several boxes in different sizes, all addressed to Ellie, that I open first. The first is addressed to her formal title. When I open it, I discover fabric swatches, glasses wrapped in paper, invitations, and other party things. I set it aside for her.

The next is a larger package addressed to Ellie Wakefield. Informal. I open that one and smile. It's full of summer clothing that Ellie must have purchased online. Nothing out of the ordinary here.

I reach for the smallest of the boxes and see that it's again addressed to Ellie Wakefield. Expecting it to be more online shopping goods, I open the box.

Black, lacy lingerie spills out into my hands, and my cock twitches.

Well, this is a nice surprise. She bought some hot-as-fuck underwear. The thought of seeing her wearing it makes my cock more than twitch.

But then an envelope falls out, as well. Ellie's name is written in bold handwriting. Clearly male.

I tear it open and begin to read. With each word, my body tenses in anger. What in the actual fuck is going on?

Dearest Ellie:

Since you wouldn't reply to my texts, I thought this was a good way to prove that I know where you are. And to apologize. I'm sorry we quarreled. You know I care about you more than anything in the world. Seeing you angry destroyed me. How long are you going to punish me by being away? Please, darling. Please come home to me. I want nothing more than to feel you pressed against me once again, your sweet lips under my own, and my hands holding the firm globes of your—"

"What are you doing?"

My head whips up at the sound of Ellie's voice.

"I'm going through your mail, of course. What are *you* doing?"

"I took a break from work and came to find you."

"I'd rather you just call for me. I don't like you walking around the property alone."

"I saw Baxter," she says with a shrug. "I was perfectly safe. Oh! My clothes came."

She happily dives into the box and starts pulling out flowy dresses and colorful tops.

"I needed some new things. I didn't bring much with me from London." She glances up and then notices the lingerie on the table and frowns. "What's that?"

I pick it up and pass it to her. "See for yourself."

"It's from Paris. Sabia Rosa is an exclusive shop there. Very expensive. Where did it come from?"

I don't say a word as I pass her the letter and watch as she reads it. Her cheeks flush, and then she scowls, rolls her eyes, and crumples the letter to toss away.

"He's such a moron."

"You said he doesn't love you."

"He doesn't."

I raise a brow and point at the wadded-up letter. "Sounds like he does."

"He's clearly an odd man. He might be crazy for all I know. And he's trying to manipulate me. He thinks he can charm me with pretty knickers and words, as if that will send me running back into his arms." She shakes her head adamantly. "I never *was* in his arms, which only made him angry. He thinks I'm daft. I'm not. But, hey, I got some pretty knickers out of it. I'll wear them for you sometime."

"Fuck that." The words are harsh, even to my own ears, but I don't care. "You won't wear any of that. You'll burn it."

"Do you have any idea how much this likely cost?"

"I don't give a flying fuck how much it cost. You won't be wearing lingerie that another man bought for you when you're with me. Sell it on eBay. Regift it. I don't care. But you won't ever touch it again."

She blinks slowly, watching me. "You're jealous."

"Fuck that."

"You're completely jealous."

We could be caught at any moment. I have staff on-site, and any of them could walk in. But I stalk closer to her, cup her chin firmly, and move one inch from her face when I say, "You're damn right, I'm jealous, Princess. As long as my hands are on you, no other man will even try to get close to you. You told him no. That means *no*. So, no, I don't give a shit how much this cost.

117

You'll get rid of it. And if this guy won't leave you alone, I'll be calling the London office to have him dealt with."

"Possessive," she murmurs, watching my lips. Her eyes are dilated.

"Damn right."

I back away before I do something stupid like throw her over my shoulder, carry her up to my bedroom, and have my way with her naked body.

"Oh, this is the box I've been waiting for," she says, rooting around in the parcel with the fabric samples and glasses. "Brilliant. I'll just take these things back to my flat. I have plenty of work to do this afternoon. By the way, are you going out with Sam this evening?"

"No."

"You should go."

"I said no."

"Liam, you've been stuck to me like glue for more than a week now. I'm safe here with the staff. Take a couple of hours to enjoy your friends. That's not a request, it's an order, as I'm still the boss here while Sebastian's gone."

She winks and turns to walk back to her apartment. I watch her head down the path, her ass swaying seductively. She disappears inside the boathouse, and I turn back to the mail.

I'd actually like to go and spend some time with Sam. But I don't like the idea of leaving her. The men on my staff are all trustworthy. She'll be safe.

But no one can keep her as safe as I can.

I'm a fucking control freak.

I'm GOING. Against my better judgement, I'm going out with the guys for a couple of hours. I've given my men strict orders, and they know there will be hell to pay if even one hair on Ellie's head is out of place when I get back.

She didn't hear me walk into the boathouse and up the stairs. She's sitting at the table with her back to me, her laptop open, and the contents from the large box spread out over the surface.

"No, I want *silk*," she says, and I realize she's talking to someone on speakerphone.

"Miss, there weren't any silk options in that color," a woman says. "That was as close as we could get."

"Well, that's simply unacceptable," Ellie replies cooly. "We have one month until the event, and I'm quite sure you can find silk linens somewhere on this Earth before then. In oatmeal, not cream."

"Yes, ma'am."

"Keep me posted."

She taps her phone and then sits back with a sigh, rubbing her temples. I see her hair is disheveled.

She's wearing barely-there yoga shorts and a tank. It drives me fucking crazy when she wears that outfit.

She might as well be naked for all the good it does covering her tight little body.

"Tired?" I ask as I approach. Her head whips around, and a smile spreads over her drawn features.

"I thought you would have left by now."

"I wanted to check in before I go." I kiss the top of her head and knead her shoulders. She sighs and melts into my touch. "Rough day?"

"All of this is wrong," she murmurs. "I gave specific instructions, and they ignored me. So, they can start over."

"What's it all for? A party?"

"A gala fundraiser for the children's hospital," she murmurs and groans when my thumbs dig up her neck to the ridge on the back of her head. "And I want it to be perfect. When guests feel particularly pampered, they're more likely to donate additional money. And those kids can use every pence they can get."

"I thought everything in that box was fancy."

She smiles up at me. "Thank you. I hope you have a lovely evening with your mates."

"I'll only be gone for a couple of hours."

"Take all the time you want. I'm certainly not going anywhere, and I'm quite sure you gave your staff precise instructions for my safety."

"Maybe."

Her smile spreads wider. "See? I'm perfectly safe. Go, enjoy."

"Why are you trying so hard to get rid of me?"

"So I can invite my secret lover over and have my way with him."

When my eyes narrow and my jaw clenches, Ellie laughs and stands to give me a proper hug.

"You deserve a night off. Relax. Enjoy yourself. I'm just going to have a hot shower and watch the telly for a while."

"Be good," I whisper with my lips in her hair. "I'll see you in the morning."

She nods and blows me a kiss when I walk down the stairs and lock the door of the boathouse behind me.

"Have fun," Baxter says. He's guarding the door of the boathouse. He opted to work an extra shift, earning more money for that trip he wants to take with his wife. "Have a beer for me. It's been so long since I drank, I don't remember what it tastes like."

"You have plenty of free evenings," I remind him.

"I'm married," he says, but he's smiling. "I want to stay home with her. So, you go have fun. And if you drink too much, one of us will come and pick you up."

"I won't need a designated driver," I assure him. "See you in a few hours."

I hurry up to my car and head into town.

CHAPTER 9

I'd rather be with her.

"God, you suck at this game," I say with a cocky grin as Sam stands back from the table and his missed shot. "Some things never change."

"I'm just having an off night," Sam replies. Hanging out with my old friend and a few of the guys from the fire hall has been fun. But I can't get Ellie off my mind. I'd rather be curled up on the couch with her, watching something stupid on television, than sitting here. I've been blatantly hit on at least three times since I walked through the door.

And I'm not fucking interested.

"So, what's it like working for the royal family?" Hunter Maddox is a firefighter and another hometown boy. He's a few years younger than Sam and me, but I still remember him.

"I enjoy it." I sip the one beer I've been nursing all

evening. "It has its challenges, but at the end of the day, it's like any other security detail. The goal is the same. Keep everyone alive."

"Makes sense." Hunter nods. "That Eleanor is a beauty."

That's all it takes for my body to tense up. "She's hot," another man agrees.

"Hunter should ask her out," Sam says. "He's young, nice, quite a catch. You're totally her type." My friend glances my way, and I clearly must not have my poker face in place, because he raises a shoulder and says, "Or not."

I shrug, shake my head, and notice a group of guys come into the bar and start a pool game at a nearby table.

"You know what, guys? I think I'd better get back."

"You've only been here an hour," Sam says.

I don't know how to explain to him that I hate the noise in here, the crowd. I can't hear well. I just want to head back and do my job.

Not to mention, I want to see Ellie.

"I'll be sure to call you this week," I reply. "I'll see you soon. Nice to meet you all."

I wave and walk across the room, stopping by Ty Sullivan and his friends, Josh and Zack King.

"Hey, it's good to see you, man," Ty says, holding out his hand for a shake. "You remember Josh and Zack King?"

"Of course." I shake the twin brothers' hands.

They've been familiar faces in Cunningham Falls for as long as I can remember, and Zack is one of the reasons I went into the Army in the first place.

"How are you?" Zack asks, watching me carefully.

"I'm great."

He narrows his eyes for a moment. I know he's taking my measure. He was also a Ranger, saw the same kind of scary shit that I did, and I know he's asking if I'm *okay*. But I'm not about to spill my guts here in the middle of this loud, crowded bar and tell him about the shit in my head.

It's not the time or place for that.

"Call me anytime," he says. "I mean it."

"I will. So, you all busted away from the wives to play pool?"

"We were kicked out," Josh says. "They're having book club night with some of their friends, and we aren't invited."

"I'm fine with that," Zack replies. "That's a lot of estrogen in one place."

"How's Seth?" I ask Zack. Seth is Zack's oldest son.

"He's great. He's graduating from college in the spring with a degree in environmental science. He wants to work in Glacier National Park."

"That's awesome, man."

"He's become a good man," he says, pride thick in his voice.

"Despite being a pain in the ass as a kid," Josh adds and winks. "Would you like to join us, Liam?"

"No, thanks. I'm headed back to headquarters. But it was good to see you."

"Anytime," Zack says again.

I wave and head out into the warm summer night. I parked my car just down the block. It's a good night for a walk. The sky is clear, lit up with millions of stars.

And it gives me an idea.

I hurry back to HQ and let Baxter know that I'm taking the princess off property for a bit before hurrying up the stairs and into Ellie's apartment.

She's on the couch, the TV on but muted as she reads something on her iPad.

"You're back early," she says when she hears me walk in. Her smile is sweet, like she's happy to see me. "Didn't you enjoy yourself?"

"It was good. But there's something I want to show you."

"Now?"

"Right now."

She looks down at the clothes she's wearing. "Do I need to change?"

She looks fucking wonderful just the way she is. "We won't see anyone where we're going."

"Then I guess I'm ready."

She stands, ready to go. She doesn't even ask where we're headed, she just trusts me to take care of everything.

It's a damn good feeling.

I take her hand and lead her down the stairs, but then drop it again when we're outside.

I don't want my men to know that anything unprofessional is happening.

"It's so nice out tonight," Ellie says. "Look at all of these stars."

"Hold that thought," I say as I open the car door for her. I get in and drive us out of the gate and away from town. I turn right after a few miles and head up Whitetail Mountain. Roughly five miles later, I turn again and find the spot I'm looking for.

When I park, I turn to look at Ellie. Her blue eyes are big as she stares out at the lights below.

"The town is so small and beautiful," she whispers. "This is a lovely spot."

"It's not just pretty," I admit and release my seatbelt. I turn toward her and push my fingers into her hair. "This is a famous point of interest in Cunningham Falls."

"Tell me more." She unfastens her own belt and turns toward me, her eyes glowing in the darkness. "What's so special about it?"

"Have you ever heard of Make Out Point? Most American towns have one."

"I don't think I recognize the term."

"Well, it's a place where young people go to make out. It's romantic."

"Is it?" She laughs and glances down at the town again. "I suppose the lights and stars are romantic. But if it's such a popular place, why are we the only ones here?"

"I guess everyone else is busy tonight." I drag my fingertips down her cheek. "Lucky for us, we're all alone."

"That is quite fortunate, isn't it?"

"Have I ever told you how much I love your accent?"

"I don't believe you have, no."

"I do," I reply before leaning over to kiss her lips softly. I can't get enough of the taste of her, the way she gasps every time our lips meet. She's sweet and addicting. "And I think this is a good opportunity to review what you've learned so far."

"That could be fun," she says just before I sink into her, tasting and exploring her perfect, smart little mouth. Our hands are everywhere, slipping over shoulders and arms. Finally, I slide up her tank, hitching it under her arms and exposing her bra and stomach.

"Take it off," she says, but I shake my head.

"Not yet." I kiss the skin at the edge of her bra. No nipple play this time. I want to explore her skin, discover what gives her goose bumps. She's gathering my shirt in her hands, pulling it up, but I shake my head and tug it back down again.

"I want to see you without the shirt," she says.

I'm not ready to show her those scars. Not yet. I

don't want to see the pity in her eyes or feel her recoil at the marred flesh.

"Not yet," I growl again. "Sit back and let me make you feel good."

"You always make me feel good." She bites her lip when I slide my fingers over her stomach and down to her navel. "You have brilliant hands."

"You have such soft skin." I kiss my way over her neck to her chin, and with my lips against hers, I whisper, "I'm going to kiss your stomach now. Is that okay?"

"Oh, yes. That would be lovely."

Her manners make me smile. I make my way down to her exposed stomach and lay open-mouthed kisses on her skin. She's warm and smooth, and her muscles contract at the light touch.

While my mouth worships her flesh, my hand travels over her thigh, up to her hip, and then down between her legs where she's hot. If her shorts were off, she'd be wet and slick in my hand.

God, I want that more than anything in the world.

But we'll get there.

She moans and arches into my touch, wanting so much more than just over-the-clothes petting.

"Liam, take my pants off."

"Not now."

"I'm going to be fifty by the time you get me naked."

"Maybe thirty," I reply with a grin. "Why are you so impatient?"

"Oh, I don't know. It could have something to do with the fact that I'm sexually frustrated every single day lately. Are you ever going to move faster than turtle mode?"

"Maybe."

I gently rub my thumb over the hard nub in her shorts and feel her jerk in her seat.

"Are you what they call a sadist?"

My head comes up so I can look her in the eyes. "What do you know of sadists?"

"I read. I think you like torturing me."

"Is that what I'm doing? Torturing you?"

She nods and moans when my thumb moves once more. Finally, I push harder, rub just a little faster, and watch with absolute fascination as Ellie comes apart in my arms, right here in the front seat of my car at Make Out Point.

She's panting, her hands in fists as she rides wave after wave of ecstasy.

"I'm not a sadist," I whisper into her ear. "I'm just not in a huge hurry."

She licks her lips, trying to catch her breath. "That was rather fun."

I feel my lips twitch in response. "I'm glad you enjoyed it."

STAYING the night again with Ellie isn't the best idea. In

fact, it's a horrible one. My men will start to wonder what the fuck is going on.

And that's not even the tip of the iceberg of the long list of reasons this is the worst idea I've ever had.

But when we returned to her apartment in the boathouse, and she smiled so sweetly, then took my hand and asked me to stay, I couldn't turn her down.

I'm a fucking idiot, but I couldn't leave.

So, here I am, in her bed, holding her to me as she sleeps peacefully.

Her touch, her even breathing, it soothes me. My eyes are heavy, and sleep calls seductively.

Gunfire. There's always so much damn gunfire.

"Cunningham!"

"Adams! Retreat, goddamn it! Get the fuck out of here!"

"Cunningham, where are you?"

Why can't my men see me? Hear me? I'm right here, damn it!

"Get them behind the building! Retreat!"

"I'm going to die." Beller, the private I've come to think of as a younger brother, says with tears in his eyes. "I'm going to die, Cunningham. I want to call my mom."

"There's no time," Adams yells. "We have to find Cunningham!"

None of this makes any sense. I'm right here. Why can't Adams see me?

"I don't want to die."

"You're not going to die." I pull Beller in for a hug, trying

to protect him from something that I already know is coming.

His body jerks from the gunfire, and he falls against me, crying out. "I'm hit! I'm hit!"

"It's okay." I lower him down and see the blood start to spread on the ground beneath him. But when I look back up at his face, it's not Beller.

It's Ellie.

"Save me," she pleads. Her face is dirty. Blood is smeared on her cheek and dripping out of her mouth. "I don't want to die, Liam. Save me."

Fucking hell, I have to keep her alive. I have to. I pull her against me and push against the wound in her back.

"Stay with me, baby. You're not going to die. I promise."

"Liam."

"No, you're not going to die."

"Liam."

"Keep breathing. Just breathe."

"Liam."

I jerk awake. Ellie's petting my shoulder, crooning.

"Liam, wake up. It's just a nightmare, darling. It's just a dream."

I recoil from her touch, bound out of bed, and sink to the floor, my back against the cold wall.

"Don't touch me. Stay away from me."

"Hey." She follows but doesn't touch me. She squats next to me, keeping her hands to herself. "You're okay. I'm not going to hurt you."

"I'll hurt *you*," I rasp, my heart hammering in my

chest, in my head. My God, I could hurt her in my sleep. What the fuck was I thinking, staying with her? I can't protect her like this. I can't protect her from *me.*

"Liam." She reaches out for me, but I shrink away.

"Don't touch me, Eleanor."

"All right." She holds up her hands. "I won't touch you. I promise. I'm over here."

"This isn't going to work." I swallow hard, over the cotton on my tongue. "This is a bad idea."

"Take some breaths."

"You don't get it." I push my face into my hands. I'm embarrassed and mortified that Ellie saw me like this, at my absolute fucking worst.

"Tell me then."

"I have PTSD," I say and take my hands away from my face so I can look her in the eyes. "Nightmares every night. I barely sleep, but when I do, this happens. Every time. I'm scared to death that I could hurt you, Ellie. And that's the last thing in the world I want. It can't happen. It *won't*. So, we either have to keep seeing each other only during the day, or not at all. I'll quit if you want me to."

"You won't quit." She reaches out, and I don't cower away this time when she lightly sweeps my hair off my wet forehead. "You're sopping wet with sweat."

"Your touch always calms me," I admit in the dark. "You're everything wonderful in this world that I don't deserve. And I'll be damned if I can bring myself to let you go."

"You don't have to let me go."

I tug her into my lap and cradle her to me. "I'm so sorry."

"You didn't do anything wrong, Liam. You had a nightmare." She cups my cheek and peppers the other with soft kisses. "I was just trying to pull you out of it. You were crying out, and it was heart-wrenching."

"You were dying," I confess. "In my dream, you were dying. And I couldn't save you."

"I'm right here," she insists. "I'm not going anywhere, I promise you. And neither are you. We'll figure this out."

"You're not afraid of me?"

She smiles sweetly. "No, I'm not afraid of you."

"You should be."

"You'd never hurt me." Her voice is calm and sure. I wish with all my heart that I could be that confident. She kisses my cheek again. "You have been nothing but gentle and warm. Patient and kind. Liam, *that's* who you are."

"I could hurt you without knowing that's what I'm doing, Ellie. That's just it. I would never *mean* to, but it could happen anyway because my head is a shitshow."

She hugs me close, not caring in the least that I'm dripping with sweat.

"When you woke up, you didn't try to hurt me. You recoiled from me, Liam. You're not going to hurt me. Now, come back to bed. I'll keep you safe."

"That's my line."

"You keep me safe all day. I can protect you from this. Trust me."

She stands and reaches out for my hand. I take it and rise to my feet.

"Take your shirt off."

I shake my head no, but she just waits for me to comply. Despite everything that's happened in the past half hour, I'm still not ready for her to see my scars.

So, with my eyes on hers, I peel my shirt over my head and let it drop to the floor. As we climb into bed, I make sure my back faces away from her at all times. She'll eventually see the healed wounds, but I don't have it in me tonight to explain them.

They're a roadmap of my journey in the Army. And I'm not ready to take that trip with her tonight.

CHAPTER 10

~ELLIE~

*H*e's asleep.

I lightly brush my fingers through his dark hair and watch the moonlight dance over his square jawline. Waking up to his cries of pain was heart-wrenching. I didn't know what to do. I've heard conflicting words of advice over the years. Some say you shouldn't try to wake someone who's in the middle of a nightmare, and others say you should.

All I knew in that moment was that I had to help him.

His terrified eyes as he cowered by the wall is something I won't forget anytime soon. I can't even imagine what he must have seen in his work to give him such night terrors.

But for now, I'll watch over him as he rests. Liam makes sure I'm well taken care of every day. The least I can do is return the favor at night.

Everyone deserves a good night's sleep.

"No, not now," Liam mumbles as his eyebrows lower in a scowl.

"Shh." I smooth that space between his eyes with my fingers and kiss his cheek. "You're okay, love."

He quiets, and his breathing returns to normal.

With Liam asleep, and me looking over him, I can take a moment to admire his chest. I'm grateful that he finally took his shirt off. I don't know why he's so self-conscious. His skin is smooth and tanned, and he has a tattoo over his right pectoral.

It's a shield with some kind of ornamentation inside that I can't make out in the dark.

I'll have to ask him about it sometime.

The tattoo was a surprise. When Liam's fully clothed, his skin looks unmarred.

He murmurs in his sleep again, and I drag my fingers down his cheek. He quiets and turns toward me, settling in.

Once I'm sure the storm has passed, I let down my guard and fall into sleep beside him.

THE SUN IS UP. I stretch out, expecting to come into contact with Liam's warm skin, but the bed is cool.

I open my eyes and glance around. I'm here alone, which is immediately disappointing.

I was hoping for another lesson this morning.

It's a bloody brilliant way to start the day.

When I turn over, my face brushes a piece of paper.

E-

Went for a run. Back later.

-L

I grin and hold the note to my chest. It's not exactly a carefully crafted work of poetry, and there's little warmth to the words. Still, it makes me ridiculously happy that he thought to pen the note at all, rather than just leave.

I slept lightly all night, waking often to check on Liam. From what I could see, he seemed to sleep well, which was a relief.

I pad out to the kitchen and make myself a cup of tea, then carry it with me to the bathroom. After a quick shower and minimal primping, I slip into the yoga shorts, sports bra, and tank that I've come to think of as my Montana uniform. It's comfortable, and Liam's eyes always light up when he looks me up and down while I'm in these clothes.

It's a win-win situation all around.

I've just returned to the kitchen for another cuppa when Liam climbs the stairs to my flat. His eyes find me immediately, and he stalks to me, dripping sweat from head to toe.

"I just got out of the shower." I hold up my hands in surrender, but he advances on me anyway. "Really, Liam, you're a sweaty mess."

"You didn't mind last night."

"I hadn't just taken a shower, silly."

I giggle and back away from him. His eyes are full of humor.

I love the playful side of Liam.

"So, you're saying I need a shower," he says as he reaches me, pinning me against the kitchen island without actually touching me.

"Yes."

He dips his head low and kisses my forehead.

"Do you mind if I use yours?"

"Of course, not. There are fresh towels in there."

"I'll be out in a few."

I nod and watch him walk to the bathroom. He pushes the door closed behind him, but before it shuts all the way, he yanks his shirt over his head, and I catch just a glimpse of his bare back before the door closes.

My God.

My stomach roils.

My eyes fill.

Liam.

I want to run after him and ask him what in the world happened to leave his back so scarred. I want to beg him to confide in me.

But I know he has to do all of that on his own terms, in his own way.

And showing him any pity at all will only make him cross with me.

I walk out onto the deck and take a deep breath,

clearing the shock from my mind. The lake is still this morning, the sun not yet high in the sky.

Birds chirp nearby. I can hear someone down at the boat below, most likely getting ready to take it out for the first patrols of the day.

With my head cleared, I walk back inside, just as Liam exits the bathroom, clenching a white towel around himself. His torso is bare and damp.

I want to lick him everywhere.

"Don't put any clothes on," I say, earning a lift of his eyebrow.

"Excuse me?"

"You heard me." I saunter toward him. "I like looking at you. Your chest deserves the Nobel Peace Prize."

His lips twitch with humor. "That sounds a little extreme."

"It's true." When I reach him, I lean in to place a kiss right over his heart. "If this impressive chest can't lead us all to world peace, it's no world I want to live in."

"You're sweet." He brushes my dry hair over my shoulder. "I like it when you don't wear makeup."

"Why?"

"Because you don't let just anybody see you like this, and I get to. You're fucking beautiful, Eleanor."

I smile. "Thank you. Now, it seems horribly unfair that you're standing there in barely anything at all."

Before he can say anything, I whip my tank over my head and toss it onto the floor.

"There. That's better."

His dark eyes hold mine, but his nostrils flare and his eyes narrow. "What kind of game are you playing, Princess?"

"You show me yours, and I'll show you mine."

He swallows hard. "You taking the lead isn't part of the deal."

"I'm not taking the lead; I'm just being playful with you." I make quick work of stripping out of my bra and watch as his eyes lower to my bare breasts. "Now, we're even. Why don't you take off that towel?"

"You're playing with fire here, Princess."

"Oh, I hope so." I reach for him, but to my utter surprise, he grabs me in his arms and carries me to the bedroom. "Did you just lose your towel?"

"No," he mutters as he climbs onto the bed and lays me down.

"You're very talented to be able to carry me and keep that towel in place at the same time."

"If the towel comes off, I won't be responsible for my actions."

I smile triumphantly, making him laugh.

"You'd tempt a saint, you know that?"

Before I can answer, he covers my mouth with his and sinks into me. For the first time, Liam's settled himself between my legs, and he's pressed against me, his cock hard behind the thick terrycloth of the towel.

I don't want *anything* between us. I know he's set on

these lessons, and I appreciate him taking his time with me, but...*come on.*

I brush my fingers up his sides and am about to circle around to his back, but he captures my hands and pins them over my head.

"Liam, I want to touch you."

He doesn't reply. His lips travel from my jawline, down to my chest. He's so tall and long-limbed that he can move around me easily and still keep my hands secured.

He sucks a nipple into his mouth, and I almost come undone. The sensations are incredible. Goose bumps work their way over my skin, and I feel heat roll over me.

I want him.

I *need* him.

"You're gorgeous," he whispers, blowing on my tender peak, then laving it with his tongue. "So responsive."

"Let me touch you, Liam."

He lets go of my hands, and I bury my fingers in his thick, dark hair. He groans, still licking and nibbling his way across my chest and down my abdomen.

My hand roams down to his shoulders. He pauses but doesn't take my hands away.

Feeling bolder, I brush my fingers across his upper back. He shakes his head.

"Don't touch my back, Ellie."

I pause. I don't understand. How can he *not* trust me with this?

"I want to touch you *everywhere*, Liam."

He shakes his head again. "Not the back."

I sigh, disappointed. Maybe I'm being selfish, trying to take him somewhere he's not ready to go. After all, he's been nothing but patient with me, letting me set the pace.

He deserves the same respect.

So, I move back up to his hair and feel him immediately relax. His lips roam over my stomach, paying particular attention to my navel.

Who knew a belly button was such a hot spot?

Not me.

"Liam."

"I love it when you say my name like that," he growls. He slides up me again and kisses me hard, as if he just can't help himself.

It's an incredible feeling to have a man practically mad with longing above you. Without thinking, my hands fall to his shoulders and move down his back again.

He quickly pins them on the bed beside my head.

"Not. The. Back."

"I wasn't thinking." My breath comes fast, my blood rushing through my head. "Liam, I'm just caught up in the moment, touching you."

He shakes his head and kisses my cheek.

"I saw your back," I admit with a whisper.

He stills, then moves off me to stare down at me. "What did you say?"

"I've already *seen* your back," I say again.

"What the fuck?" He pushes his hands through his hair and blows out a long breath.

"It was just a glimpse. When you went into the bathroom earlier."

"I didn't want you to see that." His voice is rough, his hands shaking. "Ever. And I damn well don't want you to touch it."

"I don't understand."

"That's right, you don't. You don't fucking understand."

"Then help me," I plead and watch as he manages to climb from the bed and find his shirt without exposing his back to me again.

"It's none of your business, Eleanor."

"Are you *kidding* me?" I yank a tank top on and turn to face him, my hands on my hips. "You know practically *everything* there is to know about me, Liam. You've done things to me—"

"Sex isn't the same." He shakes his head slowly. "I'm asking you right now to let this go."

I can't. I know I should, and keep going the way we have been, without getting our feelings involved.

I should do what he asks and just enjoy the time I have with him.

But I can't. I want him to trust me. I need Liam to trust me the same way I do him.

So, with my eyes pinned to his, I strip out of my clothes and stand before him completely nude. I turn in a circle with my hands out at my sides.

"This is me," I say. "I have dimples and scars and knobby knees, truth be told. I'm not always happy with what I see in the mirror, but here I am. All of me. And the only reason I can do this is because I *trust* you. Not just with my safety, but also with *me.* All of me. Liam, I deserve the same in return."

"You don't know what you're asking."

His eyes are fixed on the floor.

"Look at me."

His brown eyes find mine. He looks tortured. Sad. Maybe even a little scared.

"Just talk to me. Please."

He shakes his head and moves to turn away.

"If you leave right now—"

"What?" He whirls around, making me stumble back a step. "You'll what, Eleanor? Fire me? Yell at me? What?"

"I'll be so angry," I reply and lift my nose into the air. "And hurt. Don't do this. Fine, if you're not ready to talk about this, don't. But don't leave like this. It's not worth being so damn upset."

"It's not worth it to *you*," he replies, his voice softer. "Because you don't understand what you're asking of me."

"Help me understand."

He shakes his head again.

"Why are you so bloody stubborn?"

He stomps out of my bedroom, and I follow him, not giving the fact that I'm as naked as the day I was born a second thought.

"Get dressed," he demands.

"We need to talk about this."

"There's nothing to talk about."

He storms into the bathroom and emerges a few seconds later with his pants on.

"Liam."

He ignores me and, without a pause, heads for the stairs. Seconds later, the door slams shut.

He left me.

Standing here, naked, begging him to talk to me.

Well, he can just bugger right off.

I storm into the bedroom and throw on some clothes, then pace the flat in anger.

How *dare* he? I bared myself to him, and he just stormed right off? All because I want to know him better?

Preposterous.

I flop down onto the bed and bury my face in the pillow, but it still smells like Liam.

He's all around me.

And I've fallen right in love with the stubborn arse. That's what hurts the most. I'm in love with him, and he won't talk to me about something that has obviously hurt him deeply.

I sigh and sit up.

I just behaved like an idiot.

Mary, my childhood lady-in-waiting, used to tell me that I was impatient and could be unkind when I didn't get my way.

I've worked hard to change that about myself.

Until today, when I found out that Liam has secrets and wanted to know about them immediately.

Of course, he deserves the right to tell me when he feels the time is right.

But we need to talk this out. Because I can't help that I feel slighted. I have already given him so much of myself.

Liam isn't unkind or rude. He's been lovely.

And I pushed him too bloody hard.

I sigh, rub my hands over my face, and get ready to find Liam and eat a healthy dose of crow.

I push my feet into slides and walk calmly down the stairs. It wouldn't do to have any of Liam's staff see me running across the property screaming out Liam's name. They would definitely think something was going on if that were the case.

No, I need to be calm and collected. Clearheaded.

Patient.

But my steps quicken as I reach the bottom of the stairs and fling open the door, ready to search for the man I've fallen in love with.

But there he is. Right on the dock, standing not even six feet away from my door.

"You *left* me."

His shoulders slump, and he turns to look at me.

"I can't go far. You're my job."

"That's not what I meant, and you know it." My voice is soft now, and I'm full of insecurities as Liam walks toward me. He cups my cheek in his hand, not seeming to care that anyone could see us right here.

"Obviously, I couldn't leave you."

CHAPTER 11

~ELLIE~

"Come inside." I hold out my hand for his. To my relief, he takes it and walks with me inside and up the stairs to my flat. "I'm glad you couldn't go far."

"I feel like an ass. But, Ellie, you're pushing me on something that I'm not ready to talk about."

"I know." I swallow hard and kiss the back of his hand. "I owe you an apology for acting like a spoiled child who wasn't getting her way. I shouldn't have behaved like that. But I'm frustrated, Liam. Do you think there will ever be a time when you *are* ready to talk about it?"

He seems to think about that, and then with my hand still in his, he brushes past me, walking fast toward the bedroom. I have to take three steps for every one of his to keep up with him. I watch with wide eyes when he takes a deep breath, reaches over his shoulder, and fists his shirt, pulling it over his head. He drops it to the floor, sits on the edge of my bed, and looks down at the hardwood.

His back is to me. In the light of day, I can see all the horrible scars across his skin, from just below his neck all the way into his pants. He can't look at me. His head stays bowed, and for a long time, he doesn't say anything at all.

He looks so broken, so defeated. I want nothing more than to help him, to reassure him. To help put him back together again.

"I was a First Sergeant in the Army," he says slowly. His words are measured, quiet. "That's when I retired just over a year ago. I worked my ass off for that rank, Ellie. I took my job seriously. It consumed me. It was an honor to be in the United States Army, to be a part of the Rangers. When I graduated from Ranger school, I was on top of the world, despite the cuts along my back. I got those from barbed wire that we had to crawl under."

He pauses and swallows. His head is in his hands now, and I finally move my feet from where they're stuck to the floor near the doorway and crawl onto the bed behind him. I brace my hands on his unscarred shoulders.

I search his back and find what I think are the scars from the barbed wire. I gently brush the long marks with my fingertips.

"These?"

He nods, and I place a kiss over the marks. Liam's body is tense all over, all of his muscles tight under my hands.

"The wounds healed quickly, and I moved on," he continues. "For years, we trained. More kids came in behind me, and I helped train them, too. And then Baghdad happened."

His voice is so low, I can barely hear him.

"My team was sent in to assassinate a very bad man. All of this is classified, by the way."

"I won't tell anyone."

He nods once. "We were dropped by helicopter outside of the city, and we ran to the target point. We had intel on where the mark was, how long he'd been there. We had maps. We knew exactly how it was going to go down. Quick. Easy. In and out."

He scratches his scalp in agitation.

"We were ambushed."

I feel my eyes fill with tears. I'm careful not to cry out or gasp. I want him to continue the story.

But my God, the pain in his voice is almost unbearable.

"Suddenly, we were surrounded. My men were picked off like in a video game. As if the bastards had been tipped off."

"Could they have been?"

"Possibly." He flinches when I kiss a scar on his shoulder blade. But when I kiss another, he calms.

"Only Adams and I walked out alive. Well, we crawled. And we were barely alive. I had bullets up and down my back, as you can see."

"How did you survive this? How did it not kill you?"

"You were right, I'm a stubborn ass."

"You're not. You're wonderful."

"Adams is the reason I'm here," he says. "He knew what to do to stop the bleeding. He wouldn't let me sleep. He was a pain in my ass, but he got us out of there, still breathing. That was the first time."

"The *first* time? There were others?"

He nods. "There's some road rash back there. Right flank."

I lean in and kiss the roughened skin.

"Knife wounds. No one, aside from a doctor, has ever seen my back, Eleanor. *No one.*"

"I'm so sorry, Liam."

"None of it is your fault. And I'm okay. Things were getting easier until Adams swallowed that bullet. Then the dreams got scary bad again, and everything came back to me. It still haunts me."

"Of course, it does." I kiss his entire back and work my way up to his neck. "But it's not your fault, Liam. None of it is your fault. Any more than it's mine. You joined the Army because you love your country, and you wanted to do right by it. You're a brave man."

"No. I'm not."

"Yes, you are." I let the tears fall now. "You're so

brave and strong. What happened to you is the result of war, not because you're any less of a soldier."

He turns and pins me with those dark eyes of his. "Why does being with you soothe me like it does?"

"Because you're safe with me." I kiss his jawline. "And because you know I won't judge you. I'm here to support you, Liam. To care for you. And to make you feel good."

"You make me *feel*," he replies and rolls me onto my back, hovering over me. "I've been an expert at shutting off a lot. And then I met you, and now I can't stop feeling. It's not just the physical touch either."

"I know."

His hand strokes down my side and rests on my hip.

"Needing someone was never part of my plan, Eleanor."

He kisses me gently, teasing my lips with his as he slips between my legs, the way he was earlier.

He's pressed against me, moving subtly as he kisses me for all he's worth. I cradle him to me, my hands in his hair.

"Touch me."

I open my eyes as he presses his forehead against mine.

"Are you sure? I don't have to."

"Touch me," he whispers. My hands glide down over his shoulders and move to his back. He hisses in a breath and then relaxes.

It is undoubtedly the most intimate moment of my life.

"Liam."

He pulls back so he can look at my face. "Yes, baby?"

"I know you have a plan in place, and that because of your military background, you're a stickler for following that."

"But?"

"Please make love with me. Please don't stop again."

He sighs and buries his fingers in my hair. "I don't think I could stop if I wanted to."

Thank God.

"But we're going to take our time."

I can't help myself. I laugh. "Of course, we are. I would be worried if it were any other way, Liam Cunningham."

"Anything worth doing is worth doing well." He nibbles on my shoulder, pushing the strap of my tank out of his way. "And I'm going to do you *very well.*"

"Well, then. Okay."

His smile is wicked when he suddenly rolls to the side and slips my tank up over my head.

I didn't bother with a bra when I put it back on earlier, and I'm grateful when Liam's gaze rakes over my chest, heat in his dark eyes.

"I know you said earlier that you don't always love what you see in the mirror, but you're absolutely gorgeous, babe."

Before I can answer, he wraps those talented lips around a nipple and gives it a little tug. My hands are all over his back, roaming up his sides and over his shoulders before moving to his back again.

I can't stop touching him. I can't stop moving beneath him.

He's going to drive me absolutely mad.

"There are so many things I want to show you," he whispers. "I want to lick you *everywhere*. I want to find out how you like to be touched, and I want to show you how to get yourself off."

"Yes, please."

He chuckles as his hand slides down my belly to my shorts. He slips his fingers beneath the flimsy material and groans.

"Fucking hell, you're wet."

"I'm wet *all the time*."

Liam surprises me by ripping the shorts in two, right off my body, and tosses the ruined material aside.

"Wow."

"They were in my way."

"Quite right." I bite my lip, suddenly nervous at the idea of Liam seeing the most private part of me. But when he presses on my thigh, opening me wide, I tighten at the look of pure lust on his handsome face.

"Stop me, anytime."

I nod.

"Use words. I need to know that you understand

you're in control, and you can stop this at any time, Eleanor."

"I appreciate that, and thank you, but I can't imagine wanting you to stop."

He licks his lips and then places sweet, wet kisses down my torso. My hands fist in the bedsheets when he nudges his shoulders between my thighs and takes a long, deep breath.

He's going to kiss me there.

Finally!

With his hot eyes pinned to mine, he lowers his head and swipes his tongue, very gently, against my quivering flesh.

My back bows on the bed, and starlights burst behind my eyes.

Liam cradles my ass in his hands and holds me in place so he can kiss me with his lips, his tongue. He moves up over that nub that's the most sensitive, and then down to my opening. He growls and groans, making the most delicious sounds I've ever heard in my life.

All for me.

For *me*. Not Princess Eleanor.

My hands pull at his hair, at his shoulders, silently begging him to cover me with his incredible body and finally be inside me.

"Shit."

I'm pulled out of my lusty heaven by the expletive and see Liam's forehead braced on my inner thigh.

"What?"

"I don't have any condoms." He bites my flesh, reigniting my longing for him.

"I'm on the pill." I have to swallow a moan when he licks the crease of my leg. "I had bad monthly cycles when I was young."

He covers me now, hurrying to look me right in the eyes.

"I'm as clean as it gets," he promises. "I wouldn't do anything to put you at risk."

I smile and drag my fingertips down his stubbly cheek. "I know. I think we're fine, Liam."

He kisses my chin. "Before I take off my pants, are you—?"

"I'm *sure.* I've never been surer of anything in my bloody life."

He holds my gaze for a moment as if searching inside my soul for the answer he wants. And he must get it because he reaches down and unfastens his trousers, pushes them down his hips and legs, and rests the heavy length of his cock against my wetness.

"You're the sweetest thing," he whispers and starts to move his hips back and forth, very slowly and deliberately. The tip of him nudges against that nub and sends zings of pleasure down my limbs. "You're incredible."

"Please." I hitch my legs higher on his sides. "Now, please."

"I don't want to hurt you any more than I have to."

He brushes his nose against mine. "I'm sorry, sweetheart. It's going to hurt, but then it should be fucking fantastic."

I nod, not understanding in the least how it could hurt when everything he does to me feels *so bloody good.*

He captures a nipple with his forefinger and thumb, and as he worries it, he positions himself at my opening.

"Breathe," he croons. "Just breathe."

I take a deep breath, and as I'm slowly letting it out, Liam slips inside me. There's a bit of a pinch, and an uncomfortable stretching. He stops and lets me get used to him before pushing in farther.

Inch by amazing inch, he works his way in. When he's fully seated inside me, he kisses me long and slow.

"Are you okay?"

"It actually doesn't hurt too bad," I confess. "It's not comfortable, but it's not awful."

"Those aren't exactly the words a man wants to hear when he's having sex with his girl for the first time." His voice is strained, but he's smiling down at me. "After this, it'll get easier and better."

"I feel wonderful." It's not a lie. I feel sexy and desirable. And as he begins to move his hips, I feel my muscles loosen as I get used to him. And then, he drags against something that puts the zing back into my limbs, and I can't hold back the cry that slips from my lips.

"El?"

"Don't stop." I shift my hips and open my eyes in surprise at the sensations rolling through me. "Oh, my."

"I take it we're on to the good part."

"Oh, it's good. Yes, it's quite good."

"We're shooting for better than quite good."

He's moving a bit faster, but not violently so. Every sensation is new and dazzling. Different from anything I've ever experienced.

If each time gets better than this, I might die from having sex.

What a way to go, right?

He takes one of my hands, links our fingers, and pins it above my head. This is different from before. It's not because he doesn't want me to touch him.

It's another way to link us.

And it touches me right down to the bottom of my heart.

"Liam."

"God, the way you say my name." He tenses, every muscle tightening, and he groans as he shivers.

He's panting, kissing my neck, but he's not moving his hips anymore.

"I'm not sure what happened," I admit. He chuckles and sighs before kissing my cheek.

"I came. I'm sorry, you say my name in that sexy-as-fuck way, and I can't control myself."

"Really?" I'm grinning up at him, ridiculously proud of myself. "Well, that's lovely."

"Your prim accent also does things to me," he says. "And next time, I'll make it better for you. I promise."

"It was wonderful this time."

"We can do better," he says again. "Thank you for this gift."

"It's a gift for both of us, darling."

CHAPTER 12

~LIAM~

"I have to go off property for a couple of hours."

Baxter and I are in HQ. It's been twenty-four hours since I had sex with Ellie, and I'm not sure that I've recovered yet.

I know for sure I'll never get her out of my system. Even if I was with her for fifty years—which I won't be —it wouldn't be enough time.

"We have things under control here," Baxter says. "I'll let you know if there are any issues, but it's been nice and quiet since the princess arrived."

"I know it's unusual. I'm glad she's been able to stay on the down-low and avoid the media. I'll see you soon."

I didn't tell Ellie, or anyone else for that matter, where I'm going today. When I got the call this morning from Zack King, asking me to come help him with something at the Lazy K Ranch, I didn't have to think twice.

I admire Zack, and he's a soldier. Or a former one, anyway. All he has to do is say the word, and I'll help him in any way I can.

The drive out to the ranch takes about twenty minutes. Summer is in full bloom here in Northwest Montana, so I roll down the windows and enjoy the warm weather. I don't know what Zack needs from me today, but maybe it'll be a good way to get a certain princess off my mind for a little while.

I turn off the highway and onto the driveway for the ranch. Zack gave me instructions to follow the road past the old farmhouse to the house his brother, Josh, built almost a decade ago.

The drive isn't paved, but it's well maintained and free from ruts and potholes. I park in front of Josh's house in time to see Zack's son, Seth, come out of the house with a black Lab on his heels.

"Hey, Seth. You probably don't remember me. I'm Liam, an old friend of your dad's."

"Oh, hey. Yeah, Dad said you'd be coming over. He and Uncle Josh are inside. You can go on in."

"You're not staying?"

He flashes a smile that looks just like his father's and uncle's, who happen to be identical twins.

"Nah, I'm interning up in Glacier Park for the summer. I'm getting college credit for it, too."

"Good for you. Zack mentioned the other night that you're going into environmental science."

"That's right. I'm an outdoorsy kind of guy. Today, I get to hunt for bear scat and figure out what they're eating."

"Watch out for the bears while you're at it."

Seth nods and smiles down at his dog. "Sorry, Thor. Dogs aren't allowed to come to work with me."

Thor rolls onto his back, legs in the air for a good rub. His tongue lolls out of his mouth.

Seth scratches the dog's belly, then gestures for him to follow me.

"Go on with Liam, boy."

"Come on." I pat my leg, and the friendly dog immediately hurries over to me. "I'll take good care of him."

"Have a good day. See you around."

Seth waves and hops into his late-model Ford F150, then takes off down the drive.

The last time I saw him, he was just a kid, not even a teenager yet.

And now he's in college.

I shake my head, feeling damn old as I knock on the door.

"You live here! You don't have to knock on th—" A petite blonde opens the door and then smiles sheepishly. "Sorry. Thought you were Seth. I'm Cara, Josh's wife."

"Liam." I hold out my hand for hers, and she shakes

it, then steps back to welcome me inside. "Are Zack and Josh around?"

"They're out back," she says with a nod. "Zack tried to get Seth to stay, but he's too busy looking at bear poop in the Park to hang out with the likes of us. The little kids are hanging out with the grandparents this week."

She's chatting away, leading me through the open house to the kitchen.

"Which, I admit, has been nice and quiet, and it's freed up the guys to get some serious work done. You know, running a ranch this size is a full-time job."

"Do you work here?" I ask, completely mesmerized by her. She's friendly, adorable, and just...likeable. I can see why Josh snatched her up.

"Oh, no. We want the ranch to be successful." She winks and reaches into the fridge for two bottles of water and passes one to me. "I'm a teacher here in Cunningham Falls. So I'm off for the summer."

"Oh, nice."

"And you're the head of security for the royal family?"

She watches me with curious blue eyes.

"Here in Montana, yes."

"Well, it's nice to meet you. I'm surprised our paths haven't crossed before."

"I only spent summers here when I was a kid."

"Are you harassing my help?"

We turn at the sound of Zack's voice.

"I'm just getting to know him," Cara says, already walking out of the room. "It's called being friendly, Zack. You should try it sometime."

"I'm fucking friendly," Zack mutters. "Hey, man, thanks for coming over. I'm sorry for the third degree from a certain annoying sister-in-law."

"I heard that," Cara calls from down the hall where she disappeared.

"I wasn't whispering," Zack calls back with a grin. "I love to harass that woman. We're out back. Follow me."

We walk through a sliding glass door to a deck. Josh is sitting at an outdoor table with a laptop open, his face in a scowl.

"So, what's going on, guys?" I ask.

"We have fucking poachers," Josh snarls. "It's not even hunting season, and some asshole keeps coming onto our property to kill animals."

"They've got elk and moose so far," Zack adds.

"Do you have cameras?"

"No," Josh says, shaking his head. "We found the carcasses. The fucker took their heads for trophies."

I feel my blood begin to heat. Poachers are the lowest of the low. There are laws surrounding hunting for reasons, and what this jerk is doing includes trespassing.

"How can I help?"

"We're going to invest in one hell of a security system." Zack's voice is grim. "With cameras. And we need your help with what to get, who to have install it, all of that shit."

"Your operation out here is big. I'm surprised you didn't do this years ago."

"We have some cameras set up on the far side of the property, but we can't get to it quickly. We've kept things fairly simple. Hell," Josh says, standing to pace the deck. "We've survived wolves and other predators before this. But humans, *poachers*, are a whole new arena."

I nod, understanding perfectly. "A new threat means new security measures. How many acres do you have?"

"Fifty thousand, give or take," Zack says.

"That's a lot of ground to cover. What's your budget?"

"Whatever it takes to get the job done," Zack says. "How much did it cost to outfit the royals' place on the lake?"

"Four million dollars," I reply without missing a beat.

"Okay, that might be a bit high." Josh rubs the back of his neck.

"I can get you set up on a great system for half a million."

"Jesus," Zack mutters. "I want to punch this fucker in the face. He's costing us a fortune."

"Remember last summer when we had that asshole vandalize the fence on the north pasture?" Josh asks his brother. "It'll be worth the investment."

"People suck," Zack mutters.

"Oh, you have no idea how strongly I agree," I reply. "And if you're running into issues with vandalism on top of the poaching, it's worth the investment. Not to mention, you'll be able to keep tabs on livestock, as well."

"Good point," Josh says. "And the parents. We have our parents and our aunt and uncle in little houses a couple of miles from here. A camera pointing that way will help us keep tabs on them, too."

"Mom's not going to love being spied on," Zack says.

"The cameras won't record inside the homes," I remind them, "just on the outside of them. So, in case someone gets their car stuck, or if there's wildlife hanging around that you don't *want* there, you'll be able to see it."

"Mom came face to face with a mountain lion last winter," Josh says. "Okay, we're in. Who do we need to call for this?"

"You called him." I smile and take out my phone, sending messages to my contacts. "I can have this all taken care of and up and running in a week."

"Damn, you're fast."

"This is what I do. Do you think the royal family would be willing to wait a month to have their security put into place? Not likely. We can move on this, and maybe have a poacher on video by the end of next week."

"Awesome. Thanks, Liam." Josh shakes my hand. "I'd better go move some money so we can pay for this little investment. Zack, I'm headed out with the hands this afternoon to check the fences."

Zack nods, and we watch Josh pick up his laptop and head inside.

"I'll go get this in the works right away." I shift from foot to foot, suddenly feeling unsure of my next moves.

"Appreciate it," the other man says. "What else is on your mind?"

"What do you mean?"

He lifts a brow. "I wasn't born yesterday. You have something going on in your head. Might as well talk about it."

I cross my ankle over my opposite knee and sigh heavily.

"How did you manage to go through all the fucked-up things you did in the Army and then come out of it with this normal life? A wife and kids."

He blinks, thinking it over. "I fucked up a lot, I'm not going to lie. When Seth was little, I was a shitty dad. I was never home. And his mom was a piece of shit, too. Thank God she dropped him off here, and Josh and Cara took care of him until I came home."

"But you got it together."

"Eventually." He scratches his head and looks out at the horses grazing in the pasture. "Jillian is the best thing to ever happen in my life, and that's a bold statement for a man who has several kids. I love my kids,

Liam. And I think that as I get older, I'm getting better at being a dad. But Jilly saved me from myself. When you've seen the shit we've seen, the worst of mankind, the death..."

His eyes find mine, and I nod silently.

"You carry it with you. It never really goes away, Liam. I wish I could tell you otherwise, but it would be a lie. I still dream."

I feel my eyes widen in surprise.

"Not as often as I used to, but they're there. It helped to talk to Jillian about it, to let her in. Because all I was doing on my own was letting it rot me from the inside out."

I swallow hard. Jesus, I can identify with every single word.

"And the trust issues?" He shakes his head and whistles through his teeth. "I was a bastard when it came to trust, and that was partly due to the Army, and partly because of the piece of trash I'd been married to. I didn't think I deserved Jilly, to tell you the truth."

I look down at my hands.

"You don't either."

"She's a fucking *princess*." I drag my hands through my hair. "Of course, I don't deserve her."

"Is that what she says?"

"No."

"Look, this is none of my business, but you look like you could use some advice."

"Yeah." I lean in, ready to soak up every word Zack has to say.

"Don't fuck up."

I blink. "That's it?"

"It's the best advice you'll get. I don't know what to tell you about your relationship with Eleanor. But I remember the mess I made with Jilly. I hurt her, and the thought of it kills me. She didn't do anything wrong, and I was too messed up in my head to not get in my own way. Do you care about her?"

The thought of Ellie's sweet smile, her laugh, and her smart wit crosses my mind. I can't even think about how incredible she is naked and writhing beneath me.

I don't want to embarrass myself.

"Yeah, I care about her. But I already fucked up, Zack. I'm falling for a client. She's my job."

"You're a man, not a fucking robot. Is she in danger because you can't keep it in your pants?"

"No." Fuck that. Her safety is my priority. "But she's only here for a couple more weeks. Then she goes back to London and all of her responsibilities there, and I'm still here in Montana."

"So, this is a short-term fling?"

Just the thought of that sets my teeth on edge. "It's supposed to be."

"But you don't want it to be."

"I can't see a future for me with the royal family. I'm not just a commoner, I'm also a fucked-up dude who's seen more death and destruction than any one person should. I'm full of scars."

"We all have scars," he says quietly. "Even your princess. We just wear them differently. And, for the record, wounds don't make you unworthy of love. If she's who you love, no matter her family tree, you don't give up on that. Trust me. You'll regret it forever if you do."

I take a deep breath and let it out slowly.

"Thanks, man."

"Anytime. You're always welcome here, Liam. And thanks for the help with the security issue. I appreciate it."

"Anytime," I say, echoing his sentiment. "I'm happy to help. I'd better get back."

I FEEL LIGHTER since talking things out with Zack, and when I return to the lake house, I'm eager to find Ellie and kiss the fuck out of her.

But first, I have to check in with my guys.

I walk into HQ and find Baxter sitting at the video feed table with Aaron, the kid I fired weeks ago.

"What's going on?"

"I just came by because I forgot a jacket here," Aaron says. "Baxter and I were just shooting the shit."

"All right, well, have a good one."

I move to walk away, but Aaron stops me.

"Wait. Liam, I want to apologize. I know better than to fall asleep on the job. You took me on here, and I messed up the opportunity. I'm truly sorry. I'd like to prove to you that I can do better."

"I'm going to check on something outside," Baxter says and excuses himself from the room. I know that it was most likely Baxter who gave Aaron the idea of this speech.

"I need to know that I can trust you. We're not just dealing with an average security job here, man. We're protecting *lives*."

"I know." He swallows hard and looks at me with hopeful eyes. "I understand that totally, and I know I can do a good job here, Liam."

I nod once. "You can have your job back—on a probationary basis. *One* mess up, and you're out."

His face lights up as if I just told him he won a million dollars. "Yes! Thank you. When is my first shift?"

"Tomorrow night. Be here at six."

"Yes, sir."

He hurries out of the building, and Baxter comes back in.

"Must have hired him back, huh?"

"I did. I hope I don't regret it."

"Me, too. I'm the one who encouraged him to ask you."

"You just gave up Hawaii money," I remind him, making him wince.

"I know. But the kid needs to eat. I think he'll pull his head out of his ass."

"I hope so. Where's Eleanor?"

"In the boathouse."

I nod and move to the door.

"Hey, boss?"

"Yeah?" I turn back to Baxter.

"Be careful there, okay?"

I narrow my eyes. "What are you saying?"

"Nothing. Just be careful."

I leave without another word and walk down to the boathouse. So, Baxter figured it out. It doesn't surprise me since the man's as smart as they come.

He's also discreet.

I key in the code to the door of the boathouse and walk inside without knocking.

Not that she'd be able to hear me if I did. She has the music blaring through the apartment, and I can't help but smile at her music choice.

I didn't take her for a Neil Diamond fan. As *Sweet Caroline* blasts through the building, I climb the stairs and come to a stop.

There, in the kitchen, Ellie dances around the island, wearing a little sleeveless sundress. She's chopping vegetables and tossing them into a bowl as she sings along to the song.

"So good! So good!" She does a little spin and then shoves her hand into an oven mitt and opens the door, only to have smoke billowing out around her. "Oh,

blast it! Bollocks. I followed the directions to the letter."

She pulls out a pan and sets it on the counter, then opens the window above the sink. What used to be in the pan, I have no idea.

It's a black brick now.

Ellie lowers her head to her hands and kneads her temples.

"Now, I have to start over. He won't want to eat burned pork chops."

"No, he probably won't."

Her head whips up at my voice, and she scrunches up her nose adorably.

"Surprise?" She shrugs her shoulders. "I tried to make you dinner, but it seems to have backfired. The salad should still be good unless it spontaneously combusts there on the counter, which really wouldn't surprise me at this point."

"What were you making?"

"Pork chops with apple compote and salad. Oh, and scalloped potatoes. Shite! The potatoes!"

She whirls back to the oven and groans.

"They didn't survive either. Looks like it's just salad."

"I could order a pizza, and we can have both."

She smiles over at me, and I feel it all the way to my toes.

"It's a date."

CHAPTER 13

~ELLIE~

I wish I was part feline, because I want to purr when Liam touches me like this. His hands are over my shirt, cupping my breasts.

"Just take the bloody thing off," I breathe, tipping my head back to give him easier access to my neck.

"We're out in the open," he reminds me, but doesn't stop touching me. "But I'm damn grateful for this blind spot."

I smile and then bite my lip when Liam's lips close around my earlobe.

I was out here under the pergola on the dock, reading and minding my own business, when Liam came out to look for me. It's become routine now. If he can't find me in my flat, I'm usually here in this little corner that's hidden from the prying security cameras.

Liam hasn't bothered to fix it. It's our little secret.

My hands roam freely over his back, and he doesn't

even flinch anymore. The trust that's grown between us in the past week is truly wonderful. He's been more open, more vulnerable, and it's touched me deep in my heart.

Liam isn't just sexy. He's also a good man, through and through.

His lips graze my jawline, and his hand drifts farther down my stomach to glide over my shorts. To my utter surprise, he pushes a finger under the hemline and right to my hot center.

"Oh, my," I breathe, my hips moving, inviting his finger to slip inside of me. "Liam."

"God, you're sweet," he growls, but his head pops up as if he's listening.

And then I hear it, too.

"Shit," Liam mutters, jumping away from me and sitting a good five feet back.

I straighten my clothes and smooth my hair. When I glance over to where the footsteps are getting louder, I feel the smile spread over my face.

"Callum!"

I jump up and run to give my older brother a hug. He holds me close and then frowns down at me when I pull away. His gaze shifts to Liam and then moves back to me.

"What's going on here?"

"Nothing." I shake my head. "What are you doing here? Why didn't you tell me you were coming?"

"Well, then it wouldn't be a surprise, would it?"

I whip around to Liam. "Did *you* know?"

"Of course," he says with a satisfied smile. "My security spoke with his team yesterday."

"It was a plot against me." I grin at both men. "I'm so happy to see you. I didn't realize how homesick I was until I saw you."

"I'm happy to be here," Callum replies. "Have you enjoyed relaxing the way you hoped?"

"It's been wonderful," I assure him.

"I'm going to check on a few things at HQ," Liam says, leaving Callum and me alone on the dock. We settle onto the sofa, and I find myself chattering on like mad.

"How are Mum and Father? And everyone else?"

"They're doing well," he replies. "You haven't been gone that long."

So much has happened since I left London, it feels like I've been in Montana for months.

"And what have you been up to?"

Callum smiles. "I was in Paris for a couple of weeks, and then Scotland. I was supposed to go back to London, but you were on my mind, so I decided to take a little side journey."

"Yes, because Montana is on the way to London." I roll my eyes but offer him a grateful smile. "I'm so glad you came."

"I am, as well. Now, what did I really interrupt when I found you?"

I frown as if I don't know what in the world he

might be talking about. "Absolutely nothing. Really. Liam was just filling me in on some things, and it's a nice day, so we decided to have our meeting out here by the water."

He watches me silently, chewing on his lower lip.

"You're being silly," I continue, waving him off. "There wasn't anything going on."

"If you say so. I ran into Beau a few days ago."

I scowl. "What did *he* want?"

"He was asking after you, wondering if you're okay."

"I'm perfectly wonderful, not that it's any of his business. Beau is a boring, overbearing, pompous ass, and if I never see him again, it'll be too soon. He had the nerve to send me lacy knickers."

Callum cringes. "I'm sorry about that. It's my fault. I didn't know you'd broken things off with him, and he rang me up and asked where you were."

"He texted me from several different numbers, I'm sure just in case I'd blocked him. He's not *normal*." I murmur. "Beau's not a nice man, Callum. I can't believe he's your friend."

"I never said that." He holds up a hand. "He's an acquaintance, and because he was interested in you, I was kind to him. I don't know him well at all."

"Don't bother getting to know him," I reply and watch as Callum yawns. "You look like you have jet lag something awful."

"I believe I've been awake for nearly thirty hours or so. I lost count."

"Well, you can't go to sleep now, or you'll be knackered tomorrow. We should go get you some coffee. Drips & Sips is my favorite place in town."

"I usually drink tea, but I could use a coffee or two." He smiles at me. "Look at you, fitting in like a local citizen."

"I love it here," I reply honestly. It's the truth. I do love Cunningham Falls, especially my little flat above the boathouse.

I love being with Liam the most, but I'm not ready to share that with my brother quite yet. I like having Liam all to myself.

"I'm on board then," Callum says. "Show me this wonderful café of yours."

"THE WEATHER HAS BEEN INCREDIBLE," I say to my brother as Liam and David, Callum's personal security guard, drive us into town for our coffee. "It's rather warm during the day, but it cools down nicely in the evening. And there aren't many bugs to speak of."

"Sebastian probably has pest control," Callum reminds me.

"Oh, of course. I guess I hadn't thought of that."

"It's not something you typically need to worry about," Callum replies. "I'd like to go for a run this evening, if you're up for it, David."

"Of course, sir," David replies.

David has been Callum's security for roughly two years. He's young, in excellent shape, and can keep up with my athletic brother. If Callum wasn't a prince, he likely would have played rugby professionally.

He's very physically fit.

It's one of the reasons he's Britain's most eligible bachelor.

Something I enjoy ribbing him about quite often.

Liam pulls up to Drips & Sips, and we walk in. It's mid-afternoon now, so there aren't many patrons inside, which makes me happy.

We approach the counter, and I smile when Aspen turns around and sees us.

"Well, this is a nice surprise," she says, smiling at both me and Callum.

"We're in need of caffeine," I inform her and then gesture to my brother. "I believe you've met my brother, Callum."

Aspen opens her mouth to reply, but Callum shakes his head. "No, I don't think we have."

She blinks rapidly, and her smile immediately falls.

"What can I get for you?" she asks.

We order our iced coffees and some fresh cookies that Aspen just took out of the oven, then make our way to a table against the wall.

"You sit here," Callum says, pulling out the chair for me. "I want to sit over here and enjoy the view."

I sit, then turn around to see what he's looking at.

Aspen.

"Don't look at her like that," I plead. "She's my *friend*."

Callum just waggles his eyebrows. "Challenge accepted, darling baby sister."

I sigh in exasperation and turn to Liam. "Just shoot him. Go ahead, you have my permission. Make it a headshot so he doesn't suffer too badly."

Liam's lips twitch in humor, but he doesn't make a move to follow my command.

"Killjoy," I mutter. "How long are you staying?"

"I haven't decided. I might just hang out and go back to London with you for the state dinner next week."

"Not if you're going to be an arse to my friend."

"I'm *not* an arse," he says, his face showing fake insult. "I'm charming. I'm a rather interesting bloke, truth be told."

"You're ghastly," I say, shaking my head, just as Aspen brings over our coffee and cookies. "Thank you, Aspen, these look delicious."

"You're welcome," she says and pats me on the shoulder. "Just let me know if you need anything else."

"I could use something," Callum says before Aspen can turn and walk away. She sighs heavily and turns back to him. Her expression is not friendly.

"What?" she asks.

"I'd enjoy taking you out for dinner later. What do you say?"

She blinks and then taps her lips as if she's thinking

it over. "I believe it would be a cold day in hell before I ever went to dinner with the likes of you."

She offers him a fake smile and then pats my shoulder again. "Ellie, *you* let me know if you need anything."

And with that, she storms off, leaving my brother shell-shocked, and me giggling like crazy.

"I don't think I've ever seen that happen before," I say when I've caught my breath.

"Me either," Callum mutters, scowling down at his coffee.

I pull my phone out of my Chanel bag and snap a photo of my pouting brother, then tuck it away again.

"Why on earth did you do that?"

"I'm documenting this momentous occasion," I inform him. "My brother, the most eligible bachelor of Britain, was just told to bugger off by a beautiful woman."

"You're not kind, Eleanor," he says.

I turn to Liam, who's standing a few feet away with his focus on the door. "Am I unkind, Liam?"

"No, ma'am."

"See? Liam thinks I'm kind."

"He's not your brother," Callum points out.

"Thank God for that," I whisper and take a bite of my cookie. We call these biscuits, but the Americans call them cookies.

No matter what you call them, they're delicious.

Willa Hull comes into the shop with her son, Alex,

and gives us a wave when she sees us. Willa is a good friend of Nina's, and she came to London for Sebastian and Nina's wedding.

She's a wonderful businesswoman and has always been kind to me.

"You're still in town," Willa says when she approaches the table. "Alex, I'd like to introduce you to Princess Eleanor, and Prince Callum."

The little boy's eyes widen in surprise.

He looks up at his mother.

"Like, a *real* princess and prince?"

Willa nods, and Alex turns back to us and then bends in half, bowing for us.

"It's a pleasure to meet you, Your Highnesses."

He's added a fake accent to his charming welcome, making me laugh in delight.

"Well, it's a pleasure to meet you as well, Alex."

"We're just grabbing a treat before we pick Max up at the airport. He's been in California all week."

"My dad is pretty important," Alex says with pride.

"Yes, I know," I say. "I'm sure you've missed him this week."

"Yeah. We're going out on the boat tomorrow. Do you like boats?"

I share a look with Liam, remembering the last time I was on a boat and how Liam had to rescue me from drowning.

"Honestly, I'm not the biggest fan of them, but I'm sure you'll have a lovely time."

Alex nods, and Willa ruffles his hair. "Come on, we'd better go get your dad. It was good to see you, Ellie. Callum."

We wave, and Willa takes her son to place their order. I turn back to my brother, but he continues watching them. When Aspen laughs at something Willa says, Callum's eyes go round in surprise and then in shock.

He hangs his head.

"Fuck."

"What?" I turn in my seat, but I don't see anything out of the ordinary. Willa and Aspen are just chatting and laughing. "What's wrong?"

"I *do* recognize her," he says. He clears his throat and glances back up. "I slept with her last summer after she brought breakfast to Sebastian's home after the boating accident."

"Callum." I sit back and stare in horror at my brother. "You're a complete arsehole. What is *wrong* with you?"

"It's been more than a year," he says defensively. He glances over at Liam and David. "Help me out here, guys. That's a long time."

Neither replies, and I fling my foot out under the table to kick Callum in the shin.

"Hey! That hurt."

"You deserve more than that. For fuck's sake, Callum, why do you always have to sleep with my friends? Can't you ever keep it in your trousers?"

I sigh in exasperation.

"I mean, I understand that she's beautiful, and that you're a sucker for red hair, but she's my *friend.*"

"It was just a misunderstanding. I'll apologize to her."

"No, just leave it be. You've hurt her feelings enough for one day."

"Which is exactly why I have to apologize," he repeats. As Willa and Alex leave out the front door, Callum gets up from the table and walks over to where Aspen is standing behind her counter.

I don't want to miss a moment of this, so I stand and walk closer so I can hear every word.

"Aspen," Callum begins. "I owe you a big apology. I just got off the plane after being up for thirty hours, and—"

Aspen holds up a hand, making Callum's mouth stop moving.

Impressive. I've never been able to shut the man up.

"Was there something else you needed?"

"Yes, to bloody apologize," he says, but Aspen shakes her head. "I didn't mean to hurt your feelings."

"Let's get something straight," she replies. "You didn't hurt me. It takes a hell of a lot more than an egotistical, full-of-himself prince to hurt me. Besides, you don't know me, remember? What do you care?"

"Well, I—"

"That was a rhetorical question," she interrupts. I want to applaud her. Aspen is what the Americans call *badass.* "Now, if there's nothing more I can do for you, I'm closing early today."

"We're leaving," I say, pulling on Callum's arm. "Thank you, Aspen. Let's get together soon, okay?"

She smiles at me, and I'm immediately relieved that my idiot brother didn't just ruin a friendship that I've come to cherish in such a short time.

"I'd love that, Ellie. I'll text you soon."

"Lovely." I push Callum toward the door. "Let's go."

Once we're seated in the car and on our way back to the house, I look over at my sibling. He's scowling at his shoes.

"You deserved that."

"I know."

"You're still an arse."

"I know."

CHAPTER 14

~LIAM~

"Someone could walk right up on us," she whispers and then sighs when I lick along the ridge of her collarbone. Goose bumps break out across her flesh, begging for my tongue.

I'm happy to oblige.

We started out by taking a leisurely walk through the garden. It sits on the other side of the main house, and is one of Ellie's favorite places, especially with the rose bushes and other flowers in full bloom. There are paths and benches to sit on, not to mention a beautiful water feature in the middle of the Aspen trees. Even I have to admit it's a nice place to unwind.

Especially if I get to kiss the hell out of Ellie at the same time.

But that leisurely walk turned sexy when she gave me one coy look and drug her hand down my arm. That was all I could take.

Callum's been here for three days, which means I haven't had much alone time with Ellie in those seventy-two hours—something that is nothing short of pure torture. But he's out on the boat today, and we finally have a few hours to ourselves.

"Aren't there cameras over here?" she asks, glancing around.

"Of course," I murmur, leaning in to lick her ear lobe. "But this happens to be another blind spot."

"I don't know that there should be so many blind spots in the security," she says and steps to her left. "That just seems irresponsible. I thought you were better at your job than that."

"Where you're standing now isn't a blind spot," I inform her with a grin and reach out for her. "Get back here, smartass."

I tug her to me and let my lips fall over hers, nipping playfully. She grips my shirt in her fists, holding on as I kiss her like my life depends on it.

Because there are moments, like right now, that it feels like it does depend on it. I can't get enough of her. For a man who's lived his entire adult life practicing patience and endurance, I don't have any of those skills when it comes to Ellie.

I crave her.

She is my biggest weakness.

And I won't have her here with me forever, so I'm indulging in every damn second I can.

I have my hand under her shirt, and my mouth on hers when we hear someone calling out.

"Ellie!"

She pulls out of my arms and stares up at me. "It's Callum," she whispers.

"He's been interrupting us all week," I grumble and take her hand when the voice gets louder and closer. "Come on."

I pull her along after me, running away from Ellie's brother. We're both laughing and looking back, hoping he doesn't see us playing an adult game of hide and seek.

We run all the way around the house and then back to Ellie's apartment. We finally make it inside, both panting and out of breath, laughing with each other.

"That's another first," she says, leaning on the wall to catch her breath. "I've never run away from my brother before."

"I bet you've also never almost gotten caught making out with your security detail."

She pauses and tilts her head as if she has to give it some thought to remember. I reach out for her with a growl.

"Okay, you've got me there," she says, giggling again as she shoves her sweet fingers into my hair. "I've never made out with any of my security before."

"Damn right." I hoist her over my shoulder and carry her up the stairs. She slaps my ass, so I return the favor, planting the palm of my hand on the round globe of her rear end.

"Ouch." But she's giggling, so she's clearly not hurt in the least.

"You hit me first," I remind her and set her down when I get to the top of the stairs. Before I can say anything else, someone knocks loudly down below.

"Ellie!"

"What's his deal?" Ellie asks in exasperation. "Stay here. I'll go answer it."

I don't like being out of eyesight of this woman, so I stand on the stairs and watch her go to the door, my weapon ready in case anything goes sideways.

She cracks the door. "What do you want? And why are you yelling like a lunatic?"

"Let's go grab some lunch."

"Really? *That's* why you're screaming bloody murder?"

"I'm hungry."

"No." She backs away and tries to shut the door, but Callum's hand shoots out to stop her. "I'm busy, Callum."

"Fine, then." He sighs deeply, laying the guilt on thick.

"I thought you were out on the boat?" Ellie asks.

"They're calling for an afternoon thunderstorm."

Ellie nods in understanding. A storm caused Ellie and Nina's boat accident last year.

It's a moment I never want to relive.

"I came all this way to see you, and you're really going to turn me down for lunch? Let's try that diner in town. Ed's. I could use an American burger."

I can't blame him there. Ed's has the best food in town as far as I'm concerned.

She sighs and then shrugs a shoulder. "Okay. Give me fifteen to get ready, and I'll meet you up at the house."

"Brilliant."

Callum finally leaves, and Ellie shuts the door with a cringe. "I'm sorry, but he's right. He came a long way to see me."

"It's fine, sweetheart. I've had blue balls since your brother got to town, what's a few more hours?"

She wrinkles her gorgeous little nose. "What are blue balls?"

I laugh and follow her back up to the kitchen. "It's a painful condition when a man's been turned on but has no relief."

She rolls her eyes, making me grin. "Oh, please. I think you'll live. Besides, my family will do that to you. I've been living with blue balls all of my adult life."

I laugh and shake my head at her. "That's not possible, babe."

"Not from where I'm standing."

"Okay, why did everyone keep Ed's from me?" Ellie

asks once we're back in her apartment. She's rubbing her hands over her full stomach. Since the storm passed, Callum decided to go back out on the boat for the rest of the afternoon with David, his personal security. "I'm *stuffed.* But it was absolutely delicious."

"They're the best in town," I say in agreement. *Not* eating anything while on duty with Ellie was one of the hardest things I've ever done in my life. I don't usually have a problem with watching those I'm guarding eat. I'm not a junk food junkie.

But Ed's burgers are a different story altogether.

"You didn't have any," she says as if it's just occurred to her.

"I was on duty," I remind her.

"Aren't you hungry?"

"Starved, actually. I haven't eaten since breakfast."

She scowls. "Well, we could have ordered you something to go."

I watch her for a long moment. "Has it never occurred to you before that the men who look after you don't eat when you do?"

"Well, of course, they don't. It's just protocol because they're working. But I suppose it's never crossed my mind that they might be hungry. And that just makes me sound ghastly."

"No, it makes you sound like a privileged woman who's never had to think about those things. It doesn't make you a bad person."

"I've never had the kind of relationship with

someone on my staff the way I do with you. And I'm not just talking about the sex, of course." She smiles and then leans her head back on the couch, thinking it over. "I've always been friendly because I'm not a hag. Of course, I think of the staff as human beings.

"But they're also employees. So, our relationships have always been professional ones."

"Exactly," I agree.

"It's simply expected that when I'm in public being guarded, the security doesn't eat or do anything *but* make sure the royal family is safe. Because that's appropriate professionally."

"I don't disagree. I'm not complaining."

"I know, but I guess I'm just now realizing how indulged I am. I take so much of it for granted because it's all I've ever known. But you're hungry, and Callum and I ate at your favorite restaurant. I wish you'd mentioned that you'd like to take a meal to go. I wouldn't have found that inappropriate in the least. And I'm quite sure Callum would have felt the same way. We should order you some food right now."

Do I want a burger? Yes. In fact, aside from Ellie herself, there doesn't seem to be much at the moment that I want more.

"If we do that, we should order for the whole team on staff today," I reply, watching her worry her bottom lip as she thinks it over.

"Oh, that's a brilliant idea! We've done things like that in the past, and I think it's a lovely way to show appreciation. Let's do it. You go take everyone's order, and we'll go fetch it."

"This is a fun side to you," I mention as I stand and pull her to her feet. "You're a sweet woman, Eleanor."

"If I was that sweet, I would have thought to offer this when we were still there."

"I would have refused it," I reply and kiss her nose. "Because I was on duty."

"Well, then, let's get you a burger. But nothing for me because I can barely breathe."

"Why don't you come with me?"

She smiles brightly and slips her bare feet back into her sandals. "I'd love to."

I head over to HQ with her, and when we walk through the door, Baxter and Bartlett are standing at the table. They nod at me, but when they see that Ellie's with me, they both lower their heads and say, *"Your Highness."*

"We have a surprise for you," Ellie says with a smile. "We'd like to buy you a late lunch. Would cheeseburgers from Ed's Diner be okay with you?"

Both men raise their brows in surprise. "That would be fantastic," Bartlett says.

"I'm starving," Baxter adds and nods. "Thank you."

"Just write down what you'd like, and Liam and I will go fetch it for you. It's a small token of my appreciation for all you've done for me during my stay here. You always go above and beyond, and it hasn't gone unnoticed."

Bartlett and Baxter both blush, making me laugh.

"Okay, okay, their heads are big enough. Write down what you want. We'll be back soon."

"Just tell me what you want," Baxter says, reaching for a pen, "and I'll call it in so it's ready when you get there."

"Good idea. Double cheeseburger, large fries, and a chocolate shake."

"Me, too," Baxter says.

"Three of those," Bartlett adds. "And thank you, miss."

"It's entirely my pleasure."

"I THINK you're the favorite around here now," I say several hours later, after the food was fetched and devoured, and Ellie and I are back in her apartment alone.

"I do so enjoy being the favorite," she says with a smile. She's texting on her phone. "Callum's going to be out for a while. I don't know what he's up to, but he says he won't be back for a couple of hours yet."

She bats her eyelashes at me and covers my lap with her bare leg. I'm a sucker for Ellie in short-shorts.

Okay, I'm a sucker for Ellie period.

"Whatever shall we do with our time alone?" she asks.

"I guess we could play poker."

She smirks. "Or, we could play poke her."

I stare at her in surprise and then bust up laughing. "I can honestly say, I never expected something like that to come out of your sexy little mouth."

"I can be clever." She sniffs and boosts herself onto my lap, straddling me. "Why don't we go back to our lessons? I know we made it to home base already, but there must be lessons in there we skipped over."

"Several, actually."

"Do tell." She settles against me, and my cock immediately comes to life. Ellie's grin is quick and full of satisfaction. "I'm all ears."

"Well, we totally bypassed the oral lesson entirely." I easily lift her and switch our positions, laying her on the couch and kneeling next to her. "It's a very important one, too."

"We need to cover that one." She's solemn as if it's the most important thing in the world.

Princess Eleanor cracks me up.

I bend over and put my mouth on her nipple over her tank top, watching it pucker under the white cotton.

She's not wearing a bra.

When Ellie's in private, she doesn't wear much, and it's enough to drive a man to his knees.

I drag a finger down the center of her abdomen and flick her shorts open. Without being asked, she raises her hips, urging me to help her lower the denim down her legs, and toss them over my shoulder.

Since that first encounter, we've had sex a few more times, but I haven't had her sprawled out before me like a feast since then.

It's fucking ridiculous.

Ellie lowers a hand as if she's suddenly shy, and I snatch it up, kiss her knuckles and smile at her.

"You're gorgeous."

"I'm quite exposed."

I nod, letting my eyes travel the length of her. She's in that white tank and nothing else, and I want to fucking devour her.

But I have to stick to the lesson at hand.

"Thank Christ for it. You're a sight to behold, sweetheart."

She licks her lips, bites her lower lip, and watches me as I lean in to press a kiss to her bare hip.

Her phone rings, but she shakes her head. "Ignore it."

I take it slow, letting my lips journey over her thighs, her lower abdomen. Everywhere *but* what I want the most.

This is still new for her, though, and I'm going to ease her into it, even if it kills me in the process.

"Liam."

And there it is, that throaty growl that sends my blood racing.

I let my hand glide up her inner thigh and brush over her slick opening. When she arches her body in invitation, I spread her legs and settle in to blow her damn mind.

Her head shoots up, and she stares down at me in absolute wonder as I lick her hot slit from her clit to her soaked opening.

She tastes like heaven. And the noises she makes? Those breathy, high-pitched moans of ecstasy make my already hard cock strain against my zipper even more.

I rub the tip of my nose over her clit, and when I push one finger inside of her, she explodes spectacularly, riding out an orgasm that she's likely never experienced before.

Her nipples strain against her tank.

Her hips gyrate, wanting more and more from me.

When she calms down, licks her lips once more, and looks at me with hot blue eyes, I know that I've completely lost my heart to this woman.

She's everything I never knew I needed, and never thought I'd have in my life. Even if it is only for thirty days.

It's a hell of a lot more than I deserve.

"My turn," she says, reaching for me. She turns on her side and pulls me over to her so I'm next to her head. "I don't really know what I'm doing, but I'm doing it all the same."

All she has to do is touch me, and I lose my cool.

She unfastens my jeans, and I push them down my hips so my cock bobs toward her, thick and heavy.

"Like this." I take her hand in mine and wrap it

around the shaft, showing her how I like to be touched. I let go, and she continues, watching in fascination as the skin stretches and moves with her hand.

She leans closer and tentatively sticks her tongue out, gently brushing it over the very tip. I have to fist my hands and count to twenty to keep from coming too soon.

My God, her hands are magical.

Bolder now, she wraps those pink lips around the head and, as if she were born for this, she starts to massage me with her mouth. Her hand works me, and it's the sexiest sight I've ever seen in my fucking life.

"El, you have to stop, babe."

She shakes her head and lowers her brows into a frown. She's not stopping.

"I don't want to come in your mouth."

She hums, and that's all it takes. I can't hold back. Her eyes widen, but she doesn't gag or recoil in disgust. She smiles in satisfaction, and to my complete surprise, she swallows.

It's her first time doing that, and she swallows?

"You should have stopped."

"Why?"

"Because I came in your mouth. What if you didn't like it?"

"Well, now I know. It wasn't the best thing to happen in my life, but it wasn't gross either. And it was quite fun to make you lose control like that. We'll be doing that again."

I laugh and tuck myself away as my phone rings.

"Someone's trying to reach us," I say, pulling my phone out of my pants, frowning at the display.

It's London.

"Cunningham."

"This is Bernard." The king's personal security. "The princess's presence is being requested by tomorrow evening."

"I'll have her there."

I hang up and glance at Ellie. She's still pink from her orgasm.

"I have to take you home tomorrow."

She scowls. "But I'm not supposed to leave for several days yet."

"I have orders," I reply, already feeling the bubble Ellie and I have lived in for the past three weeks bursting around me. "I'd better get over to HQ and pack a bag and brief my men. We'll leave tomorrow morning."

"I'm calling my father," she says, pulling on her shorts. "Something must be wrong."

I watch her for a moment and then cup her face in my hands and kiss her hard. Then I pull back and smile at her, even though my chest already hurts. "I'll come back down in a couple of hours. Don't go anywhere, okay?"

"Okay."

I hurry down the stairs and just step outside when I

realize that I didn't zip up. I do that and turn around to find Callum right behind me.

Fuck.

His eyebrows climb.

"So. What's going on here?"

I shake my head and move to walk past him, but his voice stops me.

"Liam."

I turn to Ellie's brother. "You know what, man? If you have questions, I suggest you ask your sister. I don't know what she's ready for you to know. What I will tell you is that it's nothing that isn't consensual."

"Be careful," he warns as I walk away. "You're about to go to the palace, and we still have guillotines around there somewhere."

I wave over my shoulder and keep walking. Callum obviously knows that we're headed back to London.

CHAPTER 15

"*Y*our Highnesses, we'll be landing in thirty minutes."

The voice of our pilot over the speaker system sounds tinny. I don't reply. Callum reaches over on his chair and presses a button.

"Thank you, Richard," he says.

Callum's never nervous. At least, I've never seen him that way in all of my almost twenty-six years. He's as sure of himself as anyone I know.

But he's nervous now. He's been fidgeting in his seat, checking the time, and muttering to himself during the whole flight.

It's very unlike him.

We're all worried.

After the call from the palace last evening, I called my father's direct line, but it was my brother, Frederick, who answered.

"What's happening?" I asked.

"I'd rather you and Callum got here first, and then we can have a family meeting together."

"Where's Sebastian?"

"He and Nina are also on their way."

I swallowed hard. Freddy sounded tired. "Is he gone?"

"No. Just get here, Eleanor."

And with that, he hung up. We left Montana first thing this morning.

Liam stayed with me last night. He held me, and even though neither of us spoke about it, we knew that our special time together was at its end.

I'm worried about my father, and I'm sad at the same time. I feel selfish for the emotion, but I can't help it.

Since boarding the plane, Liam has resumed the role of my security detail. He's been on the phone with someone at the palace, and then in conversation with David.

He's barely looked my way.

He certainly hasn't touched me.

Which, if I'm being level-headed, is the right thing to do. My brother and his security are with us, not to mention two pilots and a flight attendant.

But I already miss him. I need him to hold my hand and reassure me. To be here with me as my lover and friend, not only as my bodyguard.

London rises below us, and within minutes, we're

safely on the ground. We taxi to our hangar, and Callum and David deboard the plane ahead of us.

Before we follow, Liam pulls me aside and into his arms for a strong hug. It almost takes my breath away.

"I needed this."

"Are you okay, babe?" He rubs circles on my back. He can soothe me with just a simple touch, and I realize that it's this, right here, that I'm sad about. I'm not ready to lose it.

"No," I whisper and swallow hard, wishing we could freeze time and stay right here for an hour or two. But I know we can't. "I want to know what in the bloody hell is going on with my father, and I already miss you."

I hadn't intended to say those last few words, but they tumbled out all the same. And I'm too much of a mess to be sorry for it.

"I'm right here," he replies softly before kissing my forehead. "Phillip is still on leave with his newborn, so you're stuck with me for a while yet."

"That's not what I meant." But I'm relieved. Phillip does a wonderful job, but I'm not ready to be separated from Liam yet. Once he goes back to Montana, I don't know when I'll get to see him again.

"I know. We'll talk later, I promise. Let's go find out what's going on."

Once we're in our cars—Liam and I in one, and Callum and David in the other—we set off for the palace.

The family is at an estate that we've visited many

times over the years, not far from the airport, although it feels like it takes hours to get there. Finally, we pull through the gates and stop next to a back door. I don't wait for anyone to open the car door for me. I hurry around the bonnet and inside, where Frederick and his wife, Anne, are waiting for us.

"Where is he?" I demand. Callum joins us and sets his hand on my shoulder.

"He's resting," Anne says. Her eyes are tired. Freddy looks exhausted, as well. "Your mother's with him."

"And Sebastian?" Callum asks.

"They just arrived," Freddy says and holds his arms out for me. I walk into them and hug him tightly. "It's going to be okay, little one."

"You've scared us all."

"Trust me, we've all been scared. Come into the parlor, and I'll fill you all in. Sebastian and Nina are waiting for us."

We walk through the ancient home to a large parlor that's already set up for afternoon tea, which I decline.

I hurry to Sebastian and hug him, then Nina. I see Liam out of the corner of my eye where he stands with David, Nick, and the other members of security across the room. They murmur to each other, and then his brown eyes shoot to mine.

This isn't going to be good news.

"Okay, we're all here," Sebastian says impatiently, refusing to sit down. "Talk to us."

Freddy swallows hard. "Last night at about eleven,

Father fell in the bathroom. He'd had a shower and was dressed for bed. We think he just finished brushing his teeth and was about to walk into the bedroom. Mum heard him fall."

"He hit his head," Anne continues, holding Freddy's hand as she talks. "On the edge of the vanity."

"Oh, my," Nina whispers, covering her mouth.

"Of course, the medical staff was called right in. He has quite a bruise on the left side of his head, and he required a few stitches. The doctor says he has a mild concussion."

"Why did he fall?" Sebastian asks.

"Heart attack."

I blink, not sure I understand.

"Pardon me?" Callum says.

"He had a heart attack," Freddy repeats. "It wasn't a massive one, and after an angioplasty and a stent, he shouldn't need additional surgery. He will, however, have to change some of his lifestyle habits, including his diet and exercise, but he's going to make a full recovery."

"He's been resting comfortably," Anne continues. "Your mother hasn't left his side, bless her heart."

"Has this gone out to the press?" Sebastian asks as he paces the room.

"No," Freddy says. "We're going to give it a day or so before we release any statements. I don't want to give false information."

"Good idea," Nina says with a nod.

"When can I see him?" I stand, ready to run up to the bedroom right now.

"You can see him now."

I spin at my mother's voice and hurry to her, wrapping her in my arms. She cradles me close and kisses my cheek.

"Oh, my darling girl."

"I'm so sorry, Mum."

"He's going to be okay." She kisses my forehead and pulls back, pasting a fake smile on her lovely face. "But I'm so glad all of my children are here. And your father will be happy, too."

"I'm going up," I announce and hurry up the stairs, moving down the hall and into his room. A nurse tries to stop me, but I ignore her, searching for my father.

"Well, hello."

I feel tears well at the sound of his weak voice. I hurry over, sit near his hip, and take his hand. My father has never been one for big displays of affection, but I don't care.

He could have died.

"You've given us all quite a fright." I sniff as he reaches up to catch a tear.

"There's no need for tears, poppet."

"Yes, there is a need for tears," I say and collapse onto his chest. "What would I do if you left me? You're a young man."

"I'm in my sixties, Eleanor."

"Young," I insist. "You need to take care of yourself."

"I've already heard *your country needs you.*"

"Blast the country," I say, impatience rolling through me. "This isn't about duty. Not this time. Your *family* needs you, Father."

"I'm not going anywhere, darling."

He holds me for a long moment, just like he did when I was a child, despite having wires connected to him, and an IV in his arm.

"I love you, Daddy."

I haven't called him *Daddy* in years. He was never fond of the term, he thought it was too casual.

But he doesn't scoff or reprimand me. He simply kisses my head and pats my back.

"I love you too, poppet."

"I've told him twice that he shouldn't go," Mum says as I help her decide which tiara to wear to the state dinner tonight.

I've been home for a week, and each day, Father has grown stronger and healthier.

But we all agree that he should sit this one out.

Of course, he's stubborn and refuses to send his regards.

Mum reaches for the Queen Victoria tiara, and I nod. This has always been her favorite, and it fits her well.

As an unmarried woman, I can't wear a tiara to an official event. But I already have a favorite.

The Cartier Halo tiara is one that's always drawn my eye. Of course, when the time comes, it will be up to the Crown which tiaras I'm given to wear. Upon my death, they'll be returned to the vault for future generations of royals.

I help Mum fit the tiara on her head, and she smiles at me. "It looks like we're ready. You look lovely, darling."

I glance down at my sequined green dress and smile. It's a mermaid silhouette that hugs my curves but doesn't show too much skin.

It's skirting the line of appropriate for a member of the royal family, but Mum didn't say anything, so I assume it will work for tonight.

This is an annual dinner the palace puts on each year for the heads of state from all over the world. Everyone from the President of the United States to the Prime Minister of Israel will be here.

And Father is determined to attend, as if he didn't just have a heart attack last week.

Of course, he's not about to show weakness in front of the world's most powerful leaders. And, part of me understands that, of course.

But I wish he'd have had more time to heal.

Mother and I are escorted upstairs to the family parlor, where the rest of the family is waiting.

My sisters-in-law, Nina and Anne, look lovely in

their dresses and tiaras. And my brothers are handsome in their tuxedos.

"I must say, we're an attractive family," Mum says with a smile. She takes Father's hand, and he kisses her cheek.

"They take after you," he says and gives her a wink. "Let's go meet our guests, shall we?"

Our security is very much present but discreet. Liam is also in a tux and sticks close to me, but I don't get to walk with him on my arm, or include him as my guest.

I haven't told my family about our relationship yet. It's not that I'm embarrassed, I'm wary.

What if they don't approve?

I'd rather keep our affair to myself and enjoy it, than have it pulled out from under me.

The family is introduced as we enter the room, and we greet each of the guests.

Finally, we sit and have a meal, which is always the easiest part of the evening because I can really only talk to the people on either side of me.

I'm fantastic at small talk, after many years of coaching. But I hate it.

And once we're finished with our dinner, we mingle.

This is the part I don't love. It's boring to me, and inevitably, someone asks about my relationship status or tries to introduce me to someone *appropriate*.

"Ellie."

I turn at the sound of my name and smile at Gretchen, a woman I don't know well, but who walks in the same circles of society that I do.

I don't trust Gretchen as far as I can throw her, which isn't far. She loves to gossip, and when the mood strikes, she's happy to show her claws.

"Hello, Gretchen."

"It's lovely to see you."

We exchange air kisses and offer fake smiles.

"And you."

"Oh, your necklace is just beautiful," she says. "Is that the Queen Mary?"

"It is."

Gretchen knows a lot about royal jewelry. She'd hoped to marry one of my brothers so she could wear it herself. Sebastian was always her favorite, and she was beyond miffed when he married Nina last year.

She still has her eye on Callum.

"So, how have you been? I haven't seen you in quite some time."

"I'm doing well, thank you. I was in Montana for a few weeks until recently."

"Well, that would explain it then, wouldn't it? I was so sorry to hear about you and Beauregard separating."

"There wasn't much to separate." I reach for a flute of champagne, taking it off a serving platter. I'll need a few of these if I'm to speak with this woman for long. "He and I weren't ever really together."

"I must have misunderstood." She clutches her

pearls and tries her best to look contrite, but it's all an act. "I beg your pardon."

I nod and sip my champagne, ready to move on. Liam's about six feet behind me and can hear every word of every conversation. I'd rather not talk about other men that I may or may not have been seeing when he's within earshot.

But Gretchen isn't finished.

"So, are you seeing someone new, then?" she asks.

"No." The answer is short and curt. "I've been in Montana, Gretchen. Of course, I'm not seeing anyone."

"Oh, that's right. Well, don't despair, darling. Someone will come along."

"Why on earth would I despair? I'm young, famous, and rich. I have nothing to worry about."

I wink at her and walk away, leaving her to open and close her mouth like a fish out of water.

My comment was tactless, but I was sick of listening to her. And how *dare* she pretend to pity me?

I absolutely will not stand for that.

I take a deep breath and continue around the room, chatting with some of the world's most important people while keeping an eye on my father.

He's starting to fade. His face is pale.

He should go to bed.

But he might have me beheaded if I recommend it in front of all of these people. He even refused to allow a press statement to be released on his behalf.

He said that he's fine now, and there's no need to worry the citizens.

As much as I love him, my father is as stubborn as they come.

"How are you, sweet girl?" Nina asks as she sidles up next to me.

"Tired." I smile over at her. "How was your trip to Africa?"

"The best trip I've taken in a long time. I got to see an elephant being born. I'll never forget it."

"I'm glad."

"How long have you and Liam had this thing going on?"

I frown and glance over my shoulder. Liam is scanning the room, pretending that he didn't hear Nina's question.

He heard it.

"I don't know what you're talking about."

"Sure." She grins and nudges me with her elbow. "You may be discreet, but I can feel the sexual tension from across the room."

"I haven't even spoken to him since I came into the bloody room."

"But you haven't seen the way he looks at you," she says softly. "If you ever need to talk about it, I'm here. Sebastian and I will be here for another couple of weeks."

"Thanks."

She nods and walks over to where Sebastian stands.

She slips her arm through his, and they stare lovingly at each other.

What would it feel like to have that kind of freedom with Liam? To not feel that I have to keep how I feel about him to myself?

Bloody great, that's how it would feel.

And why shouldn't I have that? Liam's a wonderful man. I'll speak with my mother later about him.

That decided, I feel lighter as I survey the room. My father has just finished posing for a group photo with all of the heads of state, and some are starting to filter out, giving the king their best wishes before they go.

Despite his health, my father will be the last to leave this party.

I want to stay and keep an eye on him, and it seems I'm not the only one. Sebastian, Freddy, and Callum are all nearby, as well.

We're a family unit, keeping vigil around our father.

Just as it should be.

CHAPTER 16

~LIAM~

*W*atching the change in Ellie over the past week has been an education.

I'm following behind her as she works the room of this state dinner. I stay a few feet away but remain close enough that I can hear conversations and can reach her within a millisecond if need be.

The likelihood is small, given the crazy amount of security in and around this place, but you never know. And that's what I'm here for.

The carefree, relaxed woman I spent the past month with has slowly melted away, taking *Ellie* with it and leaving Princess Eleanor in its place.

She's still kind and smart. Witty and sweet. But she's different. Even the way she speaks is more polished. Her shoulders are stiff and pulled back. Her movements are measured. The smile on her gorgeous face is as fake as most of the breasts in this room.

I'm not sure what to make of it yet.

I feel disconnected from her. I haven't spent much time with her. By the time I join her in her rooms at night, we're both exhausted and fall into sleep together, only to wake up the next day and start the routine all over again. I check in with the security team, and she goes about her princess duties. I know she's been in a frenzy, getting ready for her fundraiser next week.

Time is flying by.

Some of the people at this party are starting to leave, but the room is still full. Just as one person leaves Ellie, two other women show up. One, Gretchen, Ellie spoke to earlier. The other I haven't seen before.

"Eleanor," Gretchen says with a smile, "I'd like to introduce you to my friend, Vivienne."

"Oh, we've met," Ellie says and grins. "How are you, Vivienne?"

"Just splendid, thank you."

The three standing together look like something out of a magazine. Ellie is stunning with her long, blond hair twisted up at the back of her head, the green dress molding to her like a second skin.

I'll enjoy peeling it off her later.

Gretchen is taller, brunette, and has a beauty mark by her lip, Cindy Crawford style. Her dress is red, low-cut, and screams, *look at me!*

Vivienne has short, dark-blonde hair, and lots of curves outfitted in a simple black dress.

"So, Eleanor," Gretchen begins, "Vivienne and I

couldn't help but notice that your bodyguard is quite attractive."

"I believe the Americans would call him a *snack*," Vivienne adds with a giggle.

Jesus, I'm standing right fucking here. These women seem to think that anyone on the payroll is deaf and dumb.

I'm far from either.

"He's handsome, yes," Ellie says and nods.

"He'd really be the perfect one-night stand," Gretchen continues. I have to fight to keep my face expressionless.

"Clearly, he's not relationship material," Vivienne agrees. "But, goodness, look at the way he fills out that tux."

"Why wouldn't he be relationship material?" Ellie asks and sets her empty champagne flute on a tray.

"Well, the reasons are fairly obvious," Gretchen says.

"Explain them to me," Ellie says. Her face is calm, but she's gripping the back of a chair, her knuckles turning white.

"She only means that he'd be fun for a fling," Vivienne says, speaking slowly as if Ellie is stupid.

I want to throw them both out of here.

"I know what she means," Ellie replies, not looking away from Gretchen. She steps forward and gets within inches of Gretchen's face. "You're not a kind woman. I know you think you can come here, into *my* home, and judge me and everyone else here, and that no one will dare call you out on your pettiness.

"But I will. You've been baiting me all evening, and I'm done. Liam, this *snack* over here, is a kind and good man, and he doesn't deserve to listen to whatever game you're trying to play. You're a guest in *my* home, Gretchen, not the other way around. And trust me when I say you won't be invited again."

"Ellie—"

"My name is Princess Eleanor," Ellie replies coolly. "Good evening."

Ellie nods once, and we walk away from the two flummoxed women. Ellie turns to say something to me, but I shake my head once.

"Later," is all I say.

We have a lot to talk about later.

"My feet are killing me." Ellie steps out of her heels and wiggles her toes. "Being in sandals for a month was heaven. I got used to not wearing these death traps."

"They look sexy on you," I reply as I loosen my tie. "Then again, you look gorgeous in just about anything."

She offers me a tired smile. "I'm going to take a quick shower and wash this makeup off."

Wash Princess Eleanor off.

I nod. "I'm going to sit out on the patio for a few minutes, get some fresh air."

She frowns, and before she can say anything else, I take her shoulders in my hands and pull her up for a long, slow kiss.

"Go shower," I whisper. "Then come see me outside."

"All right."

She walks away, reaching behind her to unzip that sexy-as-hell dress. I'd planned to peel it off her and have my way with her this evening, but I have too much on my mind.

I walk into Ellie's kitchen and pour a glass of water, then open the French door that leads out to the private courtyard. I take a seat.

The sky is clear, but because of the light noise from London, there aren't any stars that I can see. It's a world away from Montana, that's for sure.

And that's just the sky.

I've been staying with Ellie in her apartment since we arrived. I had a talk with Charles, the head of security for the royal family, and he reluctantly allowed it. As far as I know, he hasn't told anyone else.

And I know Ellie hasn't said anything to her family yet, even Callum.

I promised her when we arrived last week that we would have a talk, but there hasn't been a free moment for it.

That ends tonight.

We need to chat.

I've just finished my water and started to relax

when Ellie walks through the doorway, looking clean and fresh in her little yoga shorts and orange tank top.

For a moment, I swore we were still in Montana.

It makes my gut tighten, and my heart ache.

I hold out my hand for hers and tug her into my lap, where she curls up and presses her face to my neck, breathing deeply.

"You smell good," I whisper before pressing a kiss to her damp hair.

"I needed to wash all of that off," she admits softly.

"Did you have a good time?"

"No." It's a short, simple answer. "I shouldn't have said those things to Gretchen."

"Which time?"

She shrugs a shoulder. "Both times. She just makes me so *angry*. Last year, she attended Nina's bridal shower and announced to her table of so-called friends, loud enough for Nina to hear, of course, that Sebastian would be *back* in her bed before long. She's a horrible person, and I hate that she's always at these events where she can spit at everyone."

"Why is she always invited?"

"She's related to someone somehow and has *Lady* before her name. I honestly don't know much about her because I've always steered clear of her. I don't trust her."

She sits up and looks me in the eyes.

"And I need to apologize to you."

"Why?" I brush her hair over her shoulder and draw

219

light circles on her chin with my thumb. "You didn't do anything wrong."

"I should have defended you more. I should have just told them that we *are* together, and I should have given her more of my wrath for implying that you're not good enough to be with me. But I don't trust them, Liam. At all. They're not good women, and they're not my friends, and it's none of their bloody business. Besides, I haven't even told my *family* about you."

"El, they're not wrong." She scowls, and I shake my head. "I'm not good enough for you."

"That's absolutely preposterous."

"Is it?" I kiss her cheek and then set her on her feet so I can stand and pace the patio. "You're Princess Eleanor Wakefield, and I'm Liam, former soldier and messed-up dude from Montana. I don't fit in this world, Ellie. Not as anything but your employee."

"You don't give yourself enough credit," she replies, propping her hands on her hips. "You're a wonderful man, and you're everything I want, Liam. I've been meaning to talk to my parents about you, but time has passed so quickly this week. But that stops now. I'm happy to shout how much I love you from the rooftops right this minute."

She takes my hand and tries to drag me behind her, but I stay rooted where I am, uttterly shell-shocked by her words.

"You what?"

"I'm going to shout it from the rooftops."

"The other part."

She narrows her eyes and then steps closer to me, dragging her hand down my chest.

"Did you think that we could go through *everything* we've been through these past few weeks and I wouldn't fall desperately in love with you?"

"El—"

"You have quickly become the best part of my life, Liam. I know it's not going to be easy, and there are more pieces to this puzzle than there would be for most people, but we can make it work. Because I've come alive since I met you, and I can't imagine my life without you. You can fit in here, or *anywhere*, as long as we stick together."

"I don't deserve you, Eleanor." I pull her against me and kiss her hard. *This* is the woman I fell for, this open, quick-to-smile, fun-loving person that has become a part of me. "I love you, too."

Her face lights up, and I feel like the luckiest man in the fucking universe.

"We can go tell my parents right now," she offers.

"Your dad's already had one heart attack, let's not wake him and give him another."

She laughs but smacks me on the arm.

"That's not funny. He won't have a heart attack. But if you hurt me, he could have you killed. You should know that now before we tell them."

I nod, enjoying the hell out of her for the first time

since we got here. "Duly noted. It's a good thing I know how to take care of myself."

She grins and moans when I sink into her lips, nibbling and devouring her the way I've wanted to all evening.

I pick her up in my arms, take her inside, and once the door is shut and locked, I carry her to the large, king-sized bed in her opulent bedroom and set her on the mattress.

This is my Ellie.

Mine.

I plant my knee on the bed and crawl over her, urging her to lay beneath me. My hands glide up her arms, and with her hands pinned over her head, I drag the tip of my tongue over her skin from the dip in her cleavage, up between her collarbones, to her neck and her mouth.

"You smell fucking amazing," I whisper.

"What do I smell like?"

"Mine." I kiss her chin. "You smell like mine, Eleanor."

I've never been in a situation where I had to sit in a room alone with a woman's father to answer questions before.

Let's be honest, I've never let it get that far with anyone. If a woman started making noises about introducing me to her family, well, that was when it was time to cut and run.

I suppose it only makes sense that my first time for this sort of thing would be with one of the most powerful men in the freaking world.

I blow out a breath, square my shoulders, and walk into the king's office.

"You asked to see me, Your Majesty."

He looks up from the papers he's reading and nods. "I did. Come, sit. Shut the door."

I do as I'm asked and sit across from the king.

I don't think I was this nervous when I was in the middle of gunfire in the Middle East.

For a long moment, Ellie's father doesn't say anything at all. He watches me with narrowed eyes the same color as his daughter's.

A lesser man would squirm.

Lucky for me, I've been in interrogation situations with the enemy and didn't crack under the pressure.

The king isn't my enemy. And he doesn't have a bullwhip in one hand, ready to crack it across my bare back.

That's a story I didn't tell Ellie. Someday, maybe.

"I had a conversation with my daughter this morning," he finally begins and sits back in his chair. "Eleanor is my *only* daughter, my youngest child, and perhaps the most headstrong of the bunch."

I smile softly. Yes, she is that.

"I was surprised that you didn't join her when she

came to speak to her mother and me about her relationship with you."

"I wanted to," I say immediately. "In fact, I would have preferred it, but she wanted to talk with you privately."

He nods. "Headstrong," he says again. "It seems you've gotten tangled up in a relationship with my daughter."

"That's one way to put it."

He raises a brow. "How would you phrase it then, Mr. Cunningham?"

"I've fallen in love with an incredible woman," I reply honestly. "For many reasons."

"Is her lineage one of them?"

"That's insulting."

"To whom?"

"To her." I lean forward. "Ellie isn't a woman who puts up with leaches. It's why she hasn't been interested in any of the men that have been paraded in front of her in the past. Because they didn't want *her*, the wonderful woman behind the Crown. They only wanted the prestige that comes with marrying into the royal family. And trust me when I tell you, they didn't hide that fact from her."

He scowls, and I keep talking.

"I don't want or need anything from you except your daughter. Just as she is. And if that means that I can't be employed by you any longer, that's fine with me, too."

He rubs his fingers over his lips. "Being part of this family is complicated. Inconvenient. And, sometimes, insulting. Once this reaches the press, you'll be hounded daily. Your life will no longer be private. Any skeletons in your closet won't just be sniffed out, they'll be put on display, on news shows and magazines. Every person you've ever been involved with, every bad decision you've ever made will come to light. If you're not ready for that, you should go back to Montana now. You won't lose your job."

I stand and walk to a window, looking out across the gardens below. Ellie's out there with her sisters-in-law, playing with her niece and nephew.

She's laughing, lifting a little girl in her arms.

With my back to her father, I start to tell him about my past in the Army, the things I saw, and the horrible acts I committed, including my time as a POW and how I murdered every single one of those men to get the fuck out of there.

I don't watch my language. I don't make it pretty or easy for him to hear.

When I finish the story, I turn to find him watching me, listening raptly.

"You see, we both have a decision to make," I say finally. "Because *this* is who she loves, sir."

"Have you told Eleanor all of this?"

"Most of it." I swallow hard. "I haven't told her about the POW camp yet."

He licks his lips. "Are you saying that I have to

decide if I want the likes of you, with your difficult past, to be with my daughter?"

I don't say anything, I just stand here solemnly, watching him.

"You haven't a legion of ex-wives with a horde of children that you've left behind. You haven't been involved in drugs, or debt, or—"

"I've killed people."

"Civilians?"

I feel my jaw tic. "No."

"Son, you were at war. Men die in war. And it sounds to me like you did what you had to do to survive."

I nod once.

"So, we're back where we started," he continues. "*You* need to think about all of this, and make a decision about being a part of Eleanor's life."

I frown.

The king sighs and stands to join me. He braces a hand on my shoulder. "You're an honorable man, Liam. You haven't said anything that would make me think that Ellie's chosen poorly. If you're happy with my daughter, and more importantly, you make *her* happy, that's all I need."

I swallow hard, relieved that, after everything I just told him, he's willing to accept me.

"Thank you, sir."

"I want all of my children to be happy. They surprise me, and sometimes, we have to adjust our expectations. I'm not an unyielding man. In fact, and don't let it get out, but I am simply that: a *man*. I love my daughter."

"And she loves you. She's been worried about you."

"She's a good girl," he says with a satisfied smile. "And a smart one, at that. If you weren't a good man, she wouldn't love you. And she certainly wouldn't fight for you. And you should know, she did just that this morning."

I swallow hard. "Thank you, sir."

He nods and pats my shoulder one last time. I leave the king's office.

Do I love Ellie? Yes, with my whole damn heart. But can I live with the princess?

That's the question.

CHAPTER 17

~LIAM~

*A*nother event. Another tux. Another evening of feeling completely out of place.

There is one difference this time, however. Tonight, for the fundraiser that Ellie's worked her ass off to plan over the past month, I'm her date.

Not security.

Her plus-one.

We've fielded questions and looks, photos and stares, all evening. Similar to the state dinner, I've stayed close to Ellie and have kept my mouth closed.

I've never been so fucking uncomfortable in my life. This tux is itchy. The food is bland. The conversation is stuffy and boring.

"It seems she took my advice," I hear Gretchen sneer to Vivienne. "I must say, if I had access to a man like that, I'd be all over him, too. Just look at his arse."

How can Ellie stand this? She's talking with another

group of women, laughing at something one of them said.

At least, I think it's a laugh. It's not a sound I've heard from her before.

Just like last week, this is a Princess Eleanor I don't know. She's rigid, formal, and fake.

And since I'm not on duty, and Phillip is just a few feet away, I decide I need a stiff drink.

"Can I get you something to drink?" I ask Ellie, who turns and smiles up at me.

"I'd love a glass of champagne. Thank you."

I nod, turn to exchange a look with Phillip, and then walk away, needing a break from the monotonous conversation and the rude comments.

I have pretty thick skin, and I give exactly zero fucks what anyone here thinks of me. That doesn't even cross my mind.

But the change in Ellie does bother me. I don't understand why she acts so differently here. She's an entirely different person than she is in private.

I walk with my drink out a side door and take a deep breath of fresh air. I just need a minute to pull it together, and then I'll stick by Ellie for as long as she wants to stay.

After all, relationships are all about compromise, right?

I only take a few drinks from the beer bottle and leave it on a table as I turn to walk back inside.

I frown at Phillip, who's standing against the wall. Ellie's nowhere in sight.

"Where the hell is she?"

"Restroom," he replies. "Just around the corner."

He should be around the corner, too, standing outside the door. I make a mental note to have a conversation with the other man later and hurry to the restroom.

I stop cold at the scene before me.

"I've told you I love you." A man is standing in front of Ellie, his arm braced on the wall next to her head. "I sent you gifts. I've thought of nothing but you for weeks. I was so worried when you disappeared, darling. You even made me resort to sending messages from different numbers, I was so desperate to reach you."

"You've got to be kidding me," Ellie mutters, shaking her head. She stares at him with pity and annoyance. She's not scared. She's not hurt. "Beau, there's no relationship here. There never was. And trying to contact me, from *any* number at all, after I specifically told you I never wanted to speak to you again, isn't just a violation of my privacy, it's absolutely creepy."

I wait, and I listen. So far, she's holding her own.

"Did you get my gift?"

"The knickers? Yes, I got it. Then I cut it up into pieces and threw it away. Because, just like you, anything you send me is garbage."

"You've always been an ungrateful little hag," he sneers. That's what I was waiting for.

"That's enough."

Beau's head comes up, and he scowls at me. "Who the fuck are you?"

"Doesn't matter," I reply. "You're bothering the princess, and you need to be on your way."

"Or what?" Beau gets in my face now, breathing hard. He smells of scotch, and his eyes are crazy.

This man is absolutely mentally unstable and shouldn't be anywhere near Eleanor.

"Or I'll escort you out."

He smirks, looks me up and down, and then it's like a lightbulb goes off over his head. "You're the security guy she's hooked up with, aren't you?"

"I'm her security," I confirm and wonder where the hell Phillip is. "And I'm telling you to leave now or be escorted out in front of the cameras for everyone to see."

"You wouldn't do that, you worthless piece of shite."

"I need backup," Phillip says behind me, and I watch as he takes Beau's elbow in his hand and drags him from the hallway. "This is the last time I escort you away from the princess, arsehole."

They disappear, and I turn back to Ellie. I'm full of anger, and I feel helpless. At Ellie's request, I didn't bring my weapon with me tonight.

Because I wasn't on duty.

I could have easily beaten the piss out of that

asshole, but that's not the point. I can't be *with* her and protect her at the same time.

"I'm so sorry you had to see that," she says. "I didn't know he would be here this evening."

"Let's go."

"I can't." She frowns at me. "Liam, I'm hosting this fundraiser. I can't leave until it's over."

"Fine. I'm going back. I'll see you when you're finished here."

"You're seriously leaving me here? I didn't do anything wrong with Beau. Nothing happened."

Frustration bubbles through me. I shake my head and push my hand through my hair.

"I know that. But I can't stay here any longer, El. I'm sorry. Enjoy the rest of the party, and I'll see you in a little while."

I wait for Phillip to return to her side, and then I leave, taking a cab back to the palace.

"THAT'S NOT how it's done here," Ellie says as soon as she walks into her apartment and toes off her shoes, losing at least five inches of height. "You don't attend an event with me and then leave *without* me. You were my escort, Liam."

I drag my hand down my face in frustration.

"Ellie—"

"You embarrassed me," she continues, fuming as she

stomps around the living space. "Gretchen and Vivienne had a marvelous time talking behind their hands and laughing at me all night."

"What do you care?" I roar, finally fed up with it all. "Why do you give a shit what those prissy bitches think of you? They're not your friends or your family."

"They'll talk," she says. "They'll spread rumors and talk to the press. I'll be dragged through the media."

"Because I left an hour early?"

"Yes!" She throws her hands in the air. "Yes, because you left me there alone, without an escort. Liam, this wasn't a birthday party for a child, or a private dinner with friends. It was a fundraising gala for a cause that I feel strongly about. I was asking those people to donate *money*. And you left."

"You're damn right I left, Eleanor. I was miserable there. Those people don't give a shit about the children's hospital. They care about being seen and having their photos taken and talking about stupid, frivolous garbage that no one cares about. I don't know how you can stand to be around those people."

She stops and stares at me. "I *am* those people, Liam."

"Tonight, you were," I agree, hating every word coming out of my mouth. This isn't how this was supposed to go. We were supposed to have a calm conversation. "I don't recognize you. I didn't last week at the state dinner, either. Princess Eleanor is a very different woman from Ellie. I'm so fucking in love with Ellie that I can't breathe without it hurting.

"Princess Eleanor? The jury's out on that one. Because what I've seen of her is *very* different from Ellie."

"What are you even *talking* about?" she asks, pacing the space. "Do you know how crazy you sound right now? I *am* Princess Eleanor."

"Well, then we have a problem."

She swallows hard, and just when I think she's going to cry, her cheeks redden with anger. "If you can't stand the sight of me doing the job I've been groomed for since the bloody day I was born, then you're right, Liam. We have a problem. I can't be the carefree, on-holiday woman you saw in Montana all of the time. I have a job. One that I rather like, actually."

I nod and walk into the closet, fetching the bag I packed as I waited for her to return from the gala.

Ellie's eyes widen when she sees me walk out again. The color that brightened her cheeks fades.

"Liam, we need to discuss this."

"It's always going to boil down to this, El. I. Don't. Fit. In. Here. It isn't your fault, or mine for that matter, we just come from two *very* different worlds. I can't do this. I'm sorry."

I walk to her and press my lips to her forehead, and then, while my feet can still carry me, I walk out of her apartment and text security to ask for a ride to the airport.

CHAPTER 18

~ELLIE~

I rush from the room, running after Liam with my heart beating out of my chest, blood rushing through my ears. I don't know which way he went, but I swing the entrance door open and frantically search up and down the dimly lit hallway.

"Your Highness."

The nighttime guard is standing nearby, frowning at me.

"Where did he go? Where is Liam?"

"He went to the front entrance of the palace, miss."

I don't stop to ask more questions, I just take off at a run, my bare feet slapping, my long ball gown flowing around me as I hurry through the palace, down steps and hallways, to the front entrance.

Please. Please let him still be here. This can't be the end of things. We need to discuss this, yell and scream at each other, and then figure it out. Isn't that how it's supposed to work?

But when I fling open the door, I see that it's no use. I'm too late. Red taillights gleaming in the darkness move away from me and disappear through the front gates before the vehicle turns on the main road and continues out of my sight.

He's gone.

Liam didn't just leave me at the gala alone, he *left me.*

I HAVEN'T LEFT my flat in three days. Food has been delivered but has remained uneaten.

I'm not hungry. I don't want to see anyone.

I've barely slept, and when I do, I dream of Liam, of being in his arms, and the ridiculously sexy things he did to my body. And then I wake up crying because I remember that he's gone.

I'm a bloody mess.

I had no idea that having a broken heart hurt this badly. That it feels like your flesh is literally being ripped from your body. That every breath is torture I wouldn't wish on my worst enemy.

Or Gretchen.

I miss him. And I'm angry with him.

Not to mention, I'm so confused! How could he go from being so loving and attentive to just...*gone?*

I was so embarrassed after he left the fundraiser. I felt abandoned, and I was the target of pitying looks. There were whispers behind hands and sympathetic smiles. But then, when I returned to the flat and found he'd already packed his bloody bag, clearly planning to leave no matter what I had to say, it felt like a slap to the face.

Who needs him, anyway?

I bite my lip and silently curse the tears that want to form. Damn it, *I* need him.

I brush the tears away and cringe when I push my fingers through my hair. It's filthy. I just haven't had the energy to wash it. Besides, no one is here to watch me wallow in self-pity.

I can stay as dirty as I like.

Suddenly, there's a knock on my door.

I frown and walk over, peep through the hole, and feel my eyebrows rise in surprise.

My mother, Anne, and Nina are here.

"Oh, darling," Mum says when I open the door and step back to let them in. "You look ghastly."

"Thank you, Mother."

"We haven't seen you in days," Nina says, also looking me over from head to toe, frowning at what she sees.

Perhaps I look worse than I thought.

"Nick told me that Liam left," Nina adds.

"Do you and your security gossip about the goings-on in the palace often?" I ask.

"Oh, yes, we talk about everyone." Nina's voice is calm but full of sarcasm. "And when I went to your mother and Anne to spread the rumors further, we decided to come and see how you're doing."

"I'm sorry," I whisper and close my eyes. "Beau was right. I'm an ungrateful hag."

"I don't think that's true," Anne says. "I think you're a woman who's recently had her heart hurt."

"Yes." I swallow hard, not wanting the tears to come back. After I watched Liam's car fade away, I started to cry, and I've barely stopped since. It's bloody irritating. "He went back to Montana."

"Did he tell you why?" Mum asks.

"Of course, he did." The tears disappear now, making room for the anger. "He said he doesn't fit in here, and that I have multiple personalities."

I glare at the window across the room.

"Can you believe that?" I continue, storming about the room. "He said that Princess Eleanor and Ellie are two completely different people, and he's not sure how he feels about the former. I've never been so insulted. Perhaps it's best that he left. I don't want that kind of negativity in my life. I want a man who loves me. *All* of me. The good and the bad. Which, let's be honest, the bad isn't all that bad, really. I'm a delightful person."

I'm on a roll, but I look at the others and see them exchanging glances.

"What?"

"Before we give you any advice or our opinions, let

me ask you some questions," Mum says as she settles on the sofa. "Did he say that he hates that you're a princess?"

I frown, thinking back on the other night. Some of it is foggy because I was so chuffed at him, I could barely think straight. I wanted to throw something at his stubborn head.

"No. He said he didn't know how to feel because the princess is so different from the woman. But—"

"Hold on," Mum says calmly. "Did he imply that he feels that way all the time? Or just when you're at public events?"

All three pairs of eyes are pinned to me, waiting for my answer.

"This all came about after the fundraiser," I admit with a sigh. "But he also asked me how I can be around *those* people, meaning the guests. I *am* those people."

"I wonder that all the time," Anne says to Nina. "Were the others kind to him? I'm sorry I had to miss the event and didn't get to see what happened."

"The women my age are awful," I reply. "And now that I think about it, most of the guests ignored him. They spoke with me and said hello when I introduced him, but they didn't engage with him much."

"Well, no wonder he feels the way he does," Nina says. "Listen, I've been around the rich and famous for most of my life. I'm used to being snubbed—or liked— based on who my family is. As a publicist, I'm also accustomed to the tabloids, and all of the ridiculousness that comes with being a public figure."

"So, you understand—"

"And none of that prepared me for being part of the royal family," she continues, interrupting me. "Ellie, Liam has never had to deal with these things. Even when he's working with one of us, he's on the periphery. No one pays attention to him, as horrible as that sounds."

"Oh, it was suggested at the state dinner that I use him as a sex toy," I say, earning shocked looks from all of them. "Right in front of him, so they were paying attention because he's handsome. It was just awful."

"He'd been here for all of two weeks when he left," Anne reminds me. "You were born into this, Ellie. This life is the norm for you. But I'll admit that for those of us who came into the royal life because of marriage, it takes some serious adjustments."

"You're right." I take a deep breath and swallow hard. "I can't expect him to adjust immediately, and I should be more patient. But to accuse me of being two different people? That's just preposterous."

"Oh, my darling Eleanor." Mum chuckles and then laughs harder when I scowl at her. "You're such an intelligent, hardworking, wonderful woman. But you're also young."

"I'm not a child."

"I didn't say 'child,'" she says. "I said *young*. Of course, you have a different persona when you're

Princess Eleanor. You have to put on a mask to keep the media and those you only know socially at arm's length. We all have to do that. And perhaps it was a disservice to you that you were groomed to behave that way and not told why, or even made aware of it."

"We all do it," Anne says softly. "If we didn't, everyone would think they're our best mates. We have to keep a thin veil in place to maintain our sanity."

"Do I really act that differently?"

"Honestly?" Nina asks. "Yeah. You do. It's something I noticed right away, and it took some getting used to. It's not so much that you're cold or have your nose in the air. I would say that you tolerate more. You hold yourself differently. Because, let's be honest, this is a business. So, perhaps saying you're more professional is a good way to phrase it. If you'd been in a private setting, and those horrible women had said those things about Liam, you would have put them in their place."

"I did anyway," I confess. "And I felt awful afterward because I knew that there could be some backlash. Those women are terrible. You remember the horrible girl from your bridal shower, the one who kept claiming that she'd been sleeping with Sebastian? Her name is Gretchen, by the way."

"I hate her," Nina says. "She's just an unhappy, jealous person. That's not your—or my—fault. Or Liam's fault, for that matter."

"And she won't be invited in the future," Mum adds,

her voice stern. "We don't tolerate that. Never have, never will."

"Are you all saying that Liam was right?" The lead ball in my stomach is growing. I start to sweat.

God, I feel awful.

"Stop torturing yourself," Nina says. "We all make mistakes. And Liam should have talked it out with you more, rather than simply running back to Montana. He's not a victim here."

"Agreed," Anne says. "Of course, you're more relaxed in private," she adds. "That's perfectly normal for anyone. And perhaps if he'd explained how he felt in a calmer manner, you could have in turn explained to him that this is simply normal life for you. But now that you're aware of it, you can pay better attention."

I stare at my wonderful sister-in-law as if she's crazy.

"Don't look at her like that," Mum says. "Relationships, all relationships, require compromise. Communication. The beginnings of love are the easiest days. It's simple to look past something we don't like because infatuation overshadows anything negative. It sounds like Liam was mature enough to see the red flags, he just didn't communicate them to you correctly."

"I'm a selfish woman," I whisper and hang my head in my hands. "Things had just been so *good*. For weeks and weeks, we were on the same page, enjoying each other. Laughing. Talking. And, suddenly, he tells me he doesn't know if he can live with a side of me that's so intrinsically who I am. It threw me for a loop."

"Threw him for one, too," Nina adds. "Because he left."

"Maybe he doesn't love me."

"He's frightened," Anne says, shaking her head. "We've all seen how he looks at you, Ellie. How sweet he is around you. Love is scary."

"It still scares the wits out of me," Mum says, surprising all of us. "And I've been married to your father for close to forty years."

"How are you all such experts in this?" I ask. "I feel lost without a map or a lifeline."

"Experience," Anne says.

"You're still learning each other," Nina adds. "It'll take a little while, but in the end, it'll be completely worth it."

"I have to go and find him." I stand and turn in a circle, unsure of where to start. "I'll call the plane and go to Montana straight away."

"No," Nina says, shaking her head and waving her hand in front of her face as if there's a bad smell. "First thing you'll do is take a shower. And wash your hair."

"And eat something," Anne adds.

"You really must shower, darling," Mum implores.

"Right. Shower, eat, and then get on the plane."

I hurry toward the bathroom and hear Anne yell out, "Don't forget to brush your teeth!"

BY THE TIME I took a shower, dried my hair, and ate, I was so exhausted from days without sleep that I fell onto the bed and slept for nine hours straight.

I was angry about losing that time, but it wouldn't have been wise to show up in Montana without my wits about me. He'd been gone for days, I figured a few more hours wouldn't hurt anything. But we left first thing this morning before the sun was even up.

Phillip is with me but hasn't said much during the flight. He's wonderful at his job, but he's never been much of a conversationalist. I had to beg him not to call ahead and tell Liam we were on our way.

The flight felt longer than ever, despite taking another nap for several hours. I ate more and stared out the window, excited to land near Cunningham Falls and rush to the lake house.

Will he be happy to see me? Will he tell me to turn around and go back to London?

Perhaps I should have called first.

But I was just too excited to *get there*. And, frankly, I want to see the look on his face when he sees me for the first time, without having the chance to prepare himself.

That first look will tell me everything I need to know.

I can only pray that he's happy to see me, and I don't leave Montana with a broken heart.

"We're landing in twenty minutes, Your Highness," the pilot says through the speaker. I reach over and push a button to reply. "Thank you."

Come on and land!

The mountains and lakes beneath the plane are absolutely gorgeous. I've been to Switzerland and Germany several times, and in my opinion, Montana is just as beautiful.

Finally, we descend lower and lower, and the wheels touch the runway.

Once we're on the ground, a car meets us, and it only takes about fifteen minutes to make it to the lake house.

I don't wait for someone to let me out. I jump out of the car and rush down to the headquarters building, pounding on the door with my fist.

It's very un-princess-like.

It only takes a moment for the door to swing open, and I'm ready with a big smile.

But it's not Liam.

"Princess Eleanor?"

"Oh, hello, Baxter. I'd like to see Liam, please."

"He's not here." Baxter frowns and looks back and forth between Phillip and me. "He left last night."

CHAPTER 19

~LIAM~

I'm putting my whole weight into it, and the fucker won't budge.

So, I shift my stance, tighten the wrench again, and push. This time, the camera doesn't only budge, the base cracks in two.

"Motherfucker." I growl and toss the wrench onto the ground, then wipe my sweaty forehead on my arm.

I'm out at the Lazy K Ranch, repairing some cameras that got damaged in a recent windstorm. These particular units are made to withstand winds of up to fifty miles per hour and extreme cold, but Mother Nature laid a doozy on us the other night.

I didn't mind it. The angry wind howling through the trees matched my mood. I've been an asshole since I returned from London. Even Baxter told me to fuck off yesterday, and he's the most level-headed man I know.

In hindsight, I know I deserved it. I was riding his ass after Zack King called to tell me that some of the cameras were down and asked if we could fix them. It wasn't Baxter's fault that Mother Nature was a bitch the other night.

It *is* my fault that this unit's base is broken in two. I'll have to order a new one and replace it later this week.

I yank my phone out of my pocket, shoot off an apologetic text to Zack, and take the camera with me. This was the last one that was down, so I get into my car and drive over the field to a nearby dirt road that will lead me past the ranch houses to the highway beyond.

Ever since I got back to town, I've regretted leaving England the way I did. I should have gotten my damn head on straight and sat Ellie down for a calm conversation, rather than speaking from a place of frustration and maybe a little fear.

I *know*, deep in my soul, that I don't deserve her. She's far too good for me, regardless of her title. She's innocent and sweet. Funny. Smart.

And I'm damaged goods. She deserves someone who hasn't been through hell and back and still carries the baggage from it.

She deserves every damn thing.

But the more I think about it, the more I realize that despite not deserving her, I can't live without her. I'm a shell of a man, snarling at those around me like a wounded bear.

Nothing like this has happened to me before. I've never experienced anything like it in my damn life. She changed me forever, and if being with her means I have to find a way to live with the constant intrusion of the press, the snide comments from strangers, and learn how to compliment Princess Eleanor as well as I do Ellie, well, then…I'll damn well do it.

Because I've been miserable since I set foot on that plane, and this is no way to live.

Now, let's hope she'll take me back. Once I grovel, apologize, and kiss her like crazy, of course.

I pull through the gate to the house, park in my usual space, and with the damaged camera in hand, walk down to HQ.

Baxter gives me the side-eye when I walk through the door.

"I'm an asshole," I say in greeting.

"Yup."

I nod once and set the camera on the table. "I need to order a new base for this."

"Were you an asshole to that, too?"

"Yeah." I open the fridge, pull out an energy drink, rip off the top, then take a long pull of it.

Before I can apologize further, there's a car on the camera that catches both of our attention.

"Who's that? Are we expecting anyone?"

"No," Baxter says, and picks up his phone to call

Bartlett, who's working the perimeter. "Yeah, vehicle at the gate. Who is it? We didn't get a call. I'll buzz it."

He hangs up the phone and pushes a button, opening the gate.

"Well?"

"It's Prince Callum," Baxter says with a shrug. "No one gave us a heads-up."

I frown and walk out the door and toward the main house. But before I can go inside, Callum rounds the building. When he sees me, he waves and jogs over.

"What's wrong?"

"No emergency," he says.

"You didn't let us know you were coming."

"It was a last-minute decision." He shrugs and gestures for me to walk with him down to the water. "Let's talk, shall we?"

"Sure." I have a hunch I know what he's here for, but I'm going to hear him out before I ask any questions.

I'm dying to ask him how she is. Surely, he's seen her in the last few days.

We reach the dock. I can't look at the boathouse. Too much happened there, and the thought of it is like a knife to the chest.

"I heard you left."

I level Callum with a gaze that says I'm not saying shit until he tells me what's on his mind.

"Give me one bloody reason why I shouldn't kick your arse."

"I can't give you a reason."

"I haven't talked to Ellie much," he says at last. "I tried to, but she wouldn't let me in. I wasn't aware that anything was wrong until she told me to bugger off through her door. She'd been crying."

"Fuck."

"So then I started asking around, and Nick said you left rather abruptly the other night."

I nod, rub my fingers over my mouth, and wait for the verbal lashing I deserve.

"You know, there's a small window of opportunity here to win her back."

"You think I'm right for your sister?"

He shakes his head and shrugs his shoulders. "It doesn't matter what I think."

"Yes, it does."

"I like you, Liam. I think you're a good guy. And from what I've seen, you genuinely make her happy— aside from the whole crying in her flat thing. You don't need my blessing."

"No, I don't. You're right."

"So, get on the bloody plane and go grovel for forgiveness, or forgive her, or whatever the blasted hell it takes to make you both happy again. Unless you've decided that you don't want her after all. In which case, I'll just bloody your nose and get on with my day."

I smirk at the thought, but Callum fists his hands, and I hold mine up in surrender.

"I want her more than I want my next breath. And you didn't have to come here to convince me of that.

I'd already decided that I was headed back to London to make it right."

"Brilliant." His shoulders relax, and he grins. "That's good news then."

"You also didn't have to make this long trip just for this conversation. We could have done this over the phone."

"Oh, I didn't, mate. This was a convenient side errand. I'm here because there's a certain café owner that I can't get out of my mind."

"Aspen?" He nods, his eyes lighting up at the mention of her name. "You have a thing for Aspen?"

"Quite a thing, yes. She hates me." His grin widens. "It's freaking brilliant. I'll wear her down eventually."

"Something tells me you don't run across women who don't like you very often."

"It's rare. I'm going to go see her and try my hand at wearing her down a bit."

"Good luck."

He places his hand on my shoulder, the same way his father had just a week ago.

"Good luck to you, mate. I think you're going to need it."

HOPPING planes back and forth between London is a pain in my ass.

The flight is long and exhausting, and it's even more

so when all I want to do is get back to Ellie. I *need* to see her.

I called ahead to let Charles and his team know that I'm on my way, so I won't have any issues getting into the palace. I haven't spoken to them since before I left last night, but everything should be in order.

I also told them not to tell Ellie that I'm coming. I need to see her face to find out if she's happy to see me, or if I've fucked up so badly that it's over for good.

Once we land and the car takes me to the palace, I hurry inside.

"Liam—" Charles says, but I wave him off.

"Later. I need to see her."

I don't let him answer as I hurry through the palace, following the same route I took less than a week ago when I ran *away*.

I pound on her door, gasping for breath. "Ellie. Open up, babe."

I pound again, but there's no answer.

Maybe she's with a member of the family.

I turn to find her and run into Nina.

"Your Highness."

"Oh, for crying out loud, Liam, it's just Nina. What are you doing here?"

"I'm looking for Ellie. Where is she? Is she with her parents?"

She frowns, looking confused. "Liam, Ellie isn't here."

"What do you mean?"

"She left first thing this morning, looking for you."

"Looking for me in *Montana*?"

"Of course."

I let my head fall back and quickly do the math. "We got on the planes at roughly the same time. She's going to get there and find out I'm not there."

"Why didn't you just call each other? Why doesn't anyone *talk* to each other in this family?"

"I wanted it to be a surprise."

"That's what *she* said." She throws her hands up into the air. "And now, you're here, and she's there, and you're no closer to fixing this."

"Thanks for the rundown." I pull my phone out of my pocket. No missed calls. So, I pull Ellie's name up and press send.

It rings twice before she answers.

"Liam?"

"Where are you?"

She's quiet for a moment, and I can't stand it.

"Ellie, I'm a little impatient right now. Tell me where you are. Please."

"I'm at the lake house."

"Stay there."

"I hadn't planned on leaving." There's my sassy girl. "And why is Callum here?"

"Ask Callum. I'm serious, Eleanor, stay exactly where you are. I'm leaving London right now."

"You're in *London*?"

"That's right. And you're not. Do. Not. Move." I

253

hang up and put the phone back in my pocket, then lean over and kiss Nina's cheek. "Thank you."

"Good luck. Tell her I said hi."

I wave and jog back to the car. I'm going to get my girl.

I'VE NEVER BEEN good at sitting still. Combine two, nine-hour flights back-to-back, and I'm like a caged animal.

I'm coming out of my skin by the time we pull through the gate of the lake house. I'm out of the car before it comes to a complete stop and immediately run down to the boathouse.

I'm positive that's where she'll wait for me.

And as I come around the corner, and the lake comes into view, I'm not disappointed. There she is, standing on the dock with her back to the water, facing me.

She's in those little yoga shorts and a red tank, her hair down and wild in the light breeze coming off the lake.

My steps slow. I don't run down to her and whisk her into my arms like they do in the movies.

I'm too raw for that.

Too heartsick.

Too fucking messed up.

Her face is solemn as I slowly walk toward her, my steps slow and measured, like a cat stalking its prey.

When I finally reach her, I cup her face in my hands, not touching her anywhere else.

"There are so many things I need to say to you, Eleanor, but nothing is as important as telling you that I love you more than anything or anyone I've loved in my life. You're the reason I breathe, and I was an idiot to walk away the way I did.

"You will *never* be away from me ever again, do you understand?"

Her eyes well with tears, and she nods slowly.

"I understand."

It's a whisper and a balm to my soul. I lower my head and kiss her softly. Before we give my men too much of a show, I pick her up, unlock the boathouse, and carry her upstairs.

I want to take her right to the bedroom, strip us both bare, and claim her in the most carnal way possible.

But some things need to be said first. I don't set her down, I sit and settle her in my lap, and she pulls away, making me frown.

"I forget myself when you hold me like this," she says and then brushes tears away. "We'll talk, and then you can hold me for as long as you like."

My arms long for the feel of her, but this is the most important conversation of my life, so I nod and wait for her to speak.

"I've had a lot of time to think," she begins. "And I understand why you were frustrated and left the way you did."

"There was no excuse for that," I disagree. "I should have talked it out with you."

"Yes." She looks me right in the eyes. "You should have. But I don't know if I would have listened. Maybe it took a few days apart for me to truly understand the situation."

She rubs her hands together and then pushes them through her hair.

"My family isn't easy. I'm used to it because I was born into it. Being a princess has been ingrained in me literally since the day I was born. It was shortsighted of me to think that you'd come to London with me and adjust in a matter of days, just because we love each other."

"Do you still love me?"

Her gaze whips to mine in surprise. "I'm here, aren't I? Do you think I would have come all this way if, at the end of this conversation, I was going to wish you well in your future endeavors?"

"I'd hope not, but you never know what people will do these days."

"Well, I wouldn't. Yes, I love you very much. And I was angry at you, but I needed to be reminded that every relationship needs communication and compromise to survive."

"Nina?"

"Along with Anne and my mum." She licks her lips. "So, while you shouldn't have left, I also wasn't sensitive to how you must have been feeling after being thrust into the life of a royal family the way you were. And for that, I'm sorry."

"You're forgiven."

She offers me a small smile and then keeps talking.

"Liam, I'd never thought of myself as having two different personas until you pointed it out. Again, because it's just always been, and I was too selfish to realize it."

"You're not selfish."

"I am." The admission is soft and self-deprecating. "But now that I know better, I can do better. Princess Eleanor, the dresses and makeup, the jewelry, it's all a mask. It's how I protect myself from those people. You've met them."

"Yes, I have." And now I feel like a bigger asshole because I should have seen it. It's my job to be observant, and I was too wrapped up in my head to see it. "And it makes total sense, El. I should have realized."

She shrugs one beautiful shoulder. "We both should have. And I should have thought to warn you. But we can *should* ourselves all day. I'm sorry for not thinking of your feelings."

"You're forgiven. Now, can I please apologize, as well?"

"You already did."

"Sort of." I reach for her, and she comes willingly

into my lap. "I love you so much I ache with it, and leaving you was pure hell. I regretted it the minute I left your apartment. I won't leave you again, not like that. If we're angry or hurt, we need to talk it through. No exceptions."

"Agreed." She cups my cheek, and I close my eyes at her sweet touch. "But, Liam, I enjoy being a princess. It may sound silly and privileged, but I'm quite fond of my family. I'm proud of my lineage, and I hope you won't ask me to give them up."

"No." I drag my fingertips down her cheek. "I wouldn't ask you to do that. I haven't been close to my parents since I went into the Army, so I sometimes forget that family is important to others. I like yours. They've been great to me, and I wouldn't ask you to walk away from them for me. That's never a choice you should have to make."

"But it makes you so uncomfortable."

"It did. You've given me a new perspective today, though. I can learn to like a tux and be nice to the mean girls."

She giggles, and I breathe a little easier now that the storm has passed. "They won't be invited to events anymore, by order of the queen."

"Really?"

"Oh, yes. She wasn't pleased when she heard how Gretchen and Vivienne behaved. They've been ostracized."

"I can't say that I'm sorry."

"I'm definitely not sorry in the least."

I take her lips, finally sinking in and kissing her the way I've longed to do. There's no time to pick her up and head for the bedroom. Ellie tugs my shirt over my head and kisses my shoulder, starting a flood of uncontrollable lust.

"You haven't touched me in days, Mr. Cunningham."

I grin against her lips as I lift her and tear the yoga shorts off her body, delighted when I find that she's not wearing underwear beneath them.

I unsheathe my cock from my pants and push up inside of her, making us both moan in pleasure. I want to take it slow, to savor every movement, but she's riding me fast, rubbing her clit against the root of my dick with every downward motion.

My eyes want to cross and roll back in my head at the same time.

"If you don't slow down, I won't last."

"Same, and it's brilliant." Her cheeks are red, her eyes glassy as she watches me, riding harder until, with my name on her lips, she succumbs to the orgasm she's been chasing.

I fall over right behind her and tug her down so I can breathe her in as I try to catch my breath.

"I don't know where you learned that one," I say, panting hard, "but I like it."

"I just made it up." Pride is thick in her voice. "I'm glad you liked it."

"I loved it." I kiss her chin. "Eleanor."

"Yes?"

"Marry me."

Her bright eyes whip to mine, hope shining through them.

"Today?"

I chuckle, wrapping my arms around her waist. "Any day you want, sweetheart. But I think you'll want to check with your father on dates. *If* that's a yes."

"Yes." She hugs me close and then kisses me hard. "A thousand times yes. It's a bloody good thing I like paperwork and can organize like nobody's business. And that you're worth it, of course."

I press my forehead to hers. "Yes, it's a bloody good thing."

EPILOGUE

~ASPEN~

*W*hat in the hell am I doing in London? Not just that, but at the freaking palace, as a guest of the royal family?

Whose life is this, anyway?

Ellie invited me to her wedding months ago, but I sort of tucked it into one of the little boxes in my head and ignored it for as long as possible—like I do with a lot of things.

I've learned that life doesn't hurt so badly if you compartmentalize.

Before I knew it, it was time to come to London to celebrate the wedding of Princess Eleanor and Liam Cunningham.

"I'm happy for them," Natasha says. She's sitting next to me, watching the newly married couple dance their first song. "The wedding was absolutely gorgeous."

"And *insane*," Monica says and nods. "I mean, eight hundred guests?"

"Just at the wedding ceremony," I remind her, watching as Liam sweeps Ellie across the floor. "There are only about a hundred people here at the reception."

"I didn't think she could top the Versace gown she wore for the ceremony," Nat says with a happy sigh. "But look at that little number."

Ellie changed into a shimmery white ballgown, perfect for a princess. Her hair is pulled back in a loose braid, and she looks so damn happy as she gazes up at her new husband, it's almost enough to make the likes of me shed a tear.

And I'm *not* a crier. I'm also not a romantic, so there's that.

"Aspen," Monica says in a loud whisper. "Ten o'clock."

I frown but see him out of the corner of my eye. Callum walks toward me, his blue eyes pinned to mine. They're hypnotic. I can't look away.

I hate him. Hate. He *forgot me.* I'd been naked, writhing beneath him, and he fucking *forgot.*

But I have to admit, he's a fine specimen of a man. I can hate him and still find him hot as hell.

"Do me the honor of a dance?"

"N—"

"Yes," Natasha says, pushing me into his arms. "Dance."

I don't have a choice. The next thing I know,

Callum has a grip on me and is whirling me around the dance floor.

"I'm not really much of a dancer."

"You're doing brilliantly," he says and touches his cheek to my temple. Holy Moses, he's too close. I remember every touch, every sigh from that night almost two years ago. The hand holding mine was in places no one had ventured in years—or since.

His body fit mine as if he were made just for me.

And he forgot.

I pull back and shake my head. "I'm not feeling well. I'd better go lie down."

"There's no reason to leave." His eyes have lost their welcome. He's cold now. "You've made yourself clear, Aspen. I won't bother you again."

And with that, he walks away, leaving me alone on the dance floor at a royal wedding.

NEWSLETTER SIGN UP

I hope you enjoyed reading this story as much as I enjoyed writing it! For upcoming book news, be sure to join my newsletter! I promise I will only send you news-filled mail, and none of the spam. You can sign up here:

https://mailchi.mp/kristenproby.com/
newsletter-sign-up

ALSO BY KRISTEN PROBY:

Other Books by Kristen Proby

The With Me In Seattle Series

Come Away With Me
Under The Mistletoe With Me
Fight With Me
Play With Me
Rock With Me
Safe With Me
Tied With Me
Breathe With Me
Forever With Me
Stay With Me
Indulge With Me
Love With Me

Coming in 2020:
Taunting Callum

Check out the full Big Sky universe here: https://
www.kristenprobyauthor.com/under-the-big-sky

Bayou Magic

Shadows

Coming in 2020:
Spells

Check out the full series here: https://www.
kristenprobyauthor.com/bayou-magic

The Romancing Manhattan Series

All the Way
All it Takes

Coming in 2020
After All

Check out the full series here: https://www.
kristenprobyauthor.com/romancing-manhattan

The Boudreaux Series

Easy Love

Easy Charm

Easy Melody

Easy Kisses

Easy Magic

Easy Fortune

Easy Nights

Check out the full series here: https://www.
kristenprobyauthor.com/boudreaux

The Fusion Series

Listen to Me

Close to You

Blush for Me

The Beauty of Us

Savor You

Check out the full series here: https://www.
kristenprobyauthor.com/fusion

From 1001 Dark Nights

Easy With You

Easy For Keeps

No Reservations

Tempting Brooke

Wonder With Me

Coming in 2020:
Shine With Me

Kristen Proby's Crossover Collection

Soaring with Fallon, A Big Sky Novel

Wicked Force: A Wicked Horse Vegas/Big Sky
Novella
By Sawyer Bennett

All Stars Fall: A Seaside Pictures/Big Sky Novella
By Rachel Van Dyken

Hold On: A Play On/Big Sky Novella
By Samantha Young

Worth Fighting For: A Warrior Fight Club/Big Sky
Novella
By Laura Kaye

Crazy Imperfect Love: A Dirty Dicks/Big Sky Novella
By K.L. Grayson

Nothing Without You: A Forever Yours/Big Sky
Novella
By Monica Murphy

Check out the entire Crossover Collection here:

https://www.kristenprobyauthor.com/kristen-proby-crossover-collection

ABOUT THE AUTHOR

Kristen Proby has published close to forty titles, many of which have hit the USA Today, New York Times and Wall Street Journal Bestsellers lists. She continues to self publish, best known for her With Me In Seattle and Boudreaux series, and is also proud to work with William Morrow, a division of HarperCollins, with the Fusion and Romancing Manhattan Series.

Kristen and her husband, John, make their home in her hometown of Whitefish, Montana with their two cats.

 facebook.com/booksbykristenproby

 instagram.com/kristenproby

 bookbub.com/profile/kristen-proby

 goodreads.com/kristenproby